DEMON
BLIND

Also by
M.J. Haag

Fairy Tale Retellings
(ALL IN THE SAME WORLD)

BEASTLY TALES

Depravity

Deceit

Devastation

TALES OF CINDER

Disowned (prequel) *

Defiant

Disdain

Damnation

RESURRECTION CHRONICLES
(hottie demons!)

Demon Ember	*Demon Night*	*Demon Fall*
Demon Flames	*Demon Dawn*	*Demon Kept* *
Demon Ash	*Demon Disgrace*	*Demon Blind* *
Demon Escape	*Demon Design* *	*Demon Defeat - 1*
Demon Deception	*Demon Discord* *	*Demon Defeat - 2*

novella

DEMON BLIND

A RESURRECTION CHRONICLES NOVELLA

M.J. HAAG

Shattered Glass
— PUBLISHING —

ISBN 978-1-63869-023-8 (eBook Edition)
ISBN 978-1-63869-025-2 (Paperback Edition)

The characters and events in this book are fictitious. Any similarities to real
persons, living or dead, are coincidental and not intended by the author.

Editing by the Proof Posse (aka Dawn, Jackie, Heather, Roxanne, Mirjam)
Cover design by Shattered Glass Publishing LLC
© Depositphotos.com

Version 2023.01.10

To everyone who needs glasses to survive.
(especially my hubby!)
I see you…even if you can't see me!
MWAHAHAHA!

RESURRECTION WORLD TIMELINE

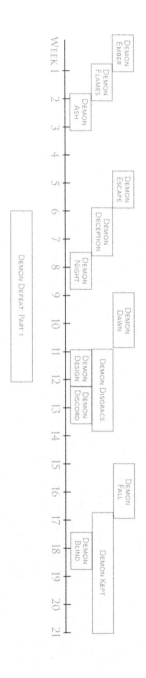

CHAPTER ONE

APRYL

I COULD SMELL THE FOOD. THE SCENT TEASED MY NOSE AND tormented my empty stomach. Sam, the young woman in front of me, shuffled forward a step. I did the same and peeked at the long blurry line that snaked down the street.

So many of us still waited to be fed. It made sense, though. Yesterday, the fey had served stew with actual meat chunks in it and warm rolls with butter. My stomach growled at the memory.

Even the threat of attracting the attention of the troublemakers, had they still been there, wouldn't have been enough to keep me away today, and it seemed like the rest of Tenacity's residents agreed. Hopefully, the fey had anticipated a bigger turnout and made enough for everyone.

"Apryl, do you see the one at the end?" Sam asked.

Tucking my chin into my poofy jacket, I kept my gaze on my feet and tugged my hat lower over my ears.

"I try not to look," I said just as one of the fey walked close to our section of the line.

I only knew it was one of them because the woman behind me shuffled away. Mentally rolling my eyes at her reaction, I hoped the fey hadn't heard what I'd said. It was my standard response whenever someone wanted me to see something. I had nothing against the fey. But I couldn't say the same for anyone else.

While the handful of survivors who outright hated the fey were gone, it didn't mean the remaining survivors were ready to welcome the fey with open arms. Just the food they brought. Hypocrites.

I didn't care that the fey kept most of the supplies collected during the supply runs since, from what I'd heard, they did all the work. And it didn't make a difference to me who was preparing our food or why the fey were actually here. They wanted women? Good for them for having a libido while the world was going to hell. Maybe that was their jam. Didn't know. Didn't care. All I cared about was keeping my head down and my mouth shut so no one would know I couldn't see shit.

"I think he's watching you."

He. One of the fey.

"They watch anything with boobs," I said, parroting what I'd been told since I'd never been able to confirm it for myself.

Sam took another step forward. "If that were true, he'd be looking at me too. This one is interested in you specifically."

"Probably my hair," I said, reaching up to make sure it was tucked into my hat. "Or my darker skin tone."

She made a humming noise, conveying her doubt.

"He hasn't glanced at Danielle once."

Danielle was darker than me, so Sam had me there.

"Are any looking at you?" I asked, redirecting the focus away from me.

Most people took a look at me and assumed I was shy because I didn't talk a lot or make eye contact. Some people, like Sam, thought striking up a conversation was being kind. It wasn't. But walking away would draw more attention to me. So I stayed put and did my best to get her talking.

"A few," she said. "But, like you said, they'll look at any female. I don't know how Brooke and Terri do it. The idea of having sex with one of the fey? No thanks. Human-sized didn't feel good. I can't imagine fey-sized."

"Not even for three meals a day and a warm place to sleep?" I asked, more than a little curious.

Since I'd heard about the housing restructuring, it was a question I'd been asking myself. Could I sleep with someone for the sake of survival? That was an easy, "Hell yes."

However, the fey were interested in women who could have their babies. And although I could physically do that, procreating wasn't something they would want me for. Not with my crappy eyesight and a world full of zombies who were getting smart enough to blend in with their surroundings. But the human men? They were a different story. They weren't interested in starting families at the end of the world. No, the threat of imminent death only solidified their need to sleep around.

"I think I already found my three meals and a warm bed," Sam said. "But without the sex." Sam shuffled forward another few steps, and I hurried to catch up.

"What do you mean?"

"You know how they're rearranging things here? I asked June if I could live with her and Tor to see what it's like living with the fey without getting anyone's hopes up."

Damn it. Why hadn't I thought of that?

"Do you think you'll still need to go out for supplies?" I asked.

Yesterday's news was causing me a fair amount of anxiety. Matt and June, our little safe haven's co-leader team, had announced more than just a change to the assigned living arrangements. They were mandating equal work contributions as well.

"I don't see why I wouldn't. They were clear that there'd be no exceptions. June said that she and Matt will be in the rotation, too, since there are two of them now."

My stomach churned and not from hunger this time.

Although Matt had been clear during the announcements that everyone would need to take a turn—no making excuses and no slacking—I'd held onto the hope that there would be exceptions. The idea of leaving the wall when I couldn't see more than a foot in front of me scared the shit out of me. The likelihood of me surviving out there was almost non-existent.

Too bad for me, obviously.

I only hoped the fey were as good at keeping people alive as Matt and June claimed.

"Do you know when they're going to announce the new schedules?" I asked Sam, hoping I'd have a few days yet.

People were currently focusing on figuring out who they wanted to live with. My housemates already thought I was a freeloader since I hadn't been able to help in any useful way. I couldn't see the wood to chop it or food to gather it, even if I was dumb enough to leave the safety of Tenacity's walls. And because of that, my housemates had made it clear I needed to find somewhere else to live.

I had a very small window of opportunity to find someone willing to take me in before the new supply run schedules started and people realized how useless I was.

"No," Sam answered. "Emily, the woman from Tolerance who's been helping coordinate the fey and human activities, has been talking to a lot of people about skills. I overheard June and Matt talking about using Emily's notes to help evenly divide talents."

"I'm not following," I said. "What does sewing have to do with getting supplies?"

"People with specialties might not be put on the supply rotation as often if they have a necessary skill. They'd be teaching instead. Emily and Matt want to ensure knowledge isn't lost. That's why Cassie is teaching her fey husband how to doctor and Mary is teaching the fey how to cook."

It wasn't enough that the fey were strong, fast, and could kill infected with little effort; they now needed to perfect human skills, too? The level of my inadequacy climbed, and I wished I had a useful skill.

"Do you think there are any other fey-human couples looking to adopt a female?" I asked.

"I don't know. You can ask Emily. She'd be happy to help you find a couple."

I almost snorted. If I showed even a hint of interest in anything fey related, she'd try setting me up with one. And I knew how the fey talked. They gossiped more than women in my granny's knitting circle. Just one slip up in front of a fey and everyone in Tolerance and Tenacity would know I was legally blind and absolute deadweight because no one wanted to pass down a genetic flaw like mine in a world full of silent danger.

The wind gusted more delicious food scents at me, distracting me from my thoughts. I inhaled deeply, acknowledging my nose was a blessing and a curse. What I'd lost in my eyes, my nose tried to make up for. Right then, though, I could have done with a nose plug. Smelling the food I couldn't yet eat but was starving for was a cruel kind of torture.

"Is the line moving slower today to you?" I asked Sam. It was my way of asking what was happening without asking it.

"Yeah, it's a little slower. I think people are trying to talk to the fey when they get up there."

"What? Why?"

Sam chuckled lightly. "Don't look so panicked. I think people are just trying to be nicer after yesterday. No one else wants to get kicked out."

"That group didn't get kicked out for forgetting to say thank you," I said.

"No. They didn't. But it doesn't hurt to be nice."

I silently disagreed with her. Being nice would hurt a lot if it resulted in anyone realizing my blindness.

I just needed to find a way to contribute before the schedules were posted and I was exposed.

CHAPTER TWO

SCATH

APRYL, THE SHY FEMALE, HAD RETURNED. SOMETHING ABOUT THE way she never looked at anyone had caught my attention when I first saw her several days ago. She kept her gaze down even when speaking to someone, which didn't happen often. I watched her, too curious about why she didn't meet anyone's gaze. Was she afraid?

Many humans were afraid for different reasons. They feared starvation, going cold, each other, and us. I sighed and wondered what her fears were. I wanted to remove them, one by one. I wanted to be the one who would earn her gaze. But how?

Fallor caught me staring at her and nudged my side.

"I think she is like Terri. You will scare her if she looks up."

"She won't look up," I said.

"Then, why stare at her?"

"She is pretty."

"There are many pretty females. Sam is one," he said, noting the female speaking with Apryl.

"She is," I said. "But Sam looks at us and smiles and has no interest in a male. Like Emily."

Fallor grunted. He had tried to gain Emily's attention many times, but she was blind to his care for her. That did not mean he had given up, only that he was waiting for her to see him.

"Now that Tor is June's, you should offer to carry Emily here when she wants to visit."

"She is not ready. She told Hannah that she wishes to see all of us with females before she opens her heart."

Fallor would be waiting a long time then since only a small number of my brothers had won females of their own, even though Tenacity had plenty of young, single women. Despite our efforts to help and show we were good, capable males, most females feared us because we were so different from them.

Self-consciously, I rubbed my pointed ear and scanned the line. However, no one appeared to be watching us, which was disappointing when my brothers and I watched the females so earnestly. A man had once said my brothers and I had the eyes of a snake, an unpleasant creature according to the few humans I'd asked. Another human said our grey skin blended too well with the shadows, making us creepy. I didn't want to be viewed as an unpleasant creeper. I wanted a female to look at me without fear in her pretty, rounded eyes.

I just wanted a female to look at me.

My gaze landed on Apryl again, and the need to see her lift her gaze to meet mine gripped me. I wanted Apryl, the female who looked at no one, to be the female who looked at me without fear. I wanted her smiles and gentle touch.

She would be mine before the moon rose tonight.

"You're starting to smile," Fallor said. "Stop."

Suppressing my triumphant grin, I checked whether any of the humans in line had noticed. Many of the humans thought we had teeth like predators, and they grew nervous if they saw us smiling. Teeth were teeth. Blunt or sharp shouldn't matter;

how we used them should. And we didn't bite people. Yet, they still feared us.

My attention drifted back to Apryl. Would she fear my teeth? I hoped not, but acknowledged she probably would.

Swallowing a disgruntled growl, I told myself to have patience. Emily was working hard to help the females lose their fear of us. Dinner dates where females would speak to us. Drawing classes where females could stare at us. Massage sessions where we could touch females.

I very much wanted to eat with a female, but not many had volunteered. A few females showed interest in the drawing classes, but only if we kept our pants on. Angel said it was because the pearl-clutchers couldn't handle the size of our equipment. I didn't know what touching jewelry had to do with my cock, but Angel was honest, and if she said we needed pants, then we did.

Watching Apryl move forward in line with the rest of the humans waiting for food, I wondered if she would volunteer for the dinner dates. She wore no ring and was considered an adult. I confirmed that by asking Matt. And she did not seem to fear us as strongly as some of the others. When Eitri had passed her, she hadn't cringed away like the woman behind her had.

That didn't mean Fallor was wrong, though. None of us had understood how deeply Terri had feared us until she began to trade with Turik. But even when Terri hadn't looked at Turik, she'd spoken to him. That was how he'd won her heart. With words.

That was a good place to start with Apryl.

"I think I will go talk to Apryl," I said to Fallor.

"I wouldn't."

"Why not?"

"She is in line for food."

"I know. That means she will not walk away from me."

"It also means that she is very hungry. Emily explained 'hangry' to us. Do you want to risk that Apryl is angry when you speak to her for the first time?"

I crossed my arms and studied her as I considered his wise words. Extreme hunger could make a woman angry in an irrational way, and I wanted Apryl to be rational when I spoke to her and told her... What should I say to her?

Females could be as easily angered by words as they could by hunger, and I didn't want to anger Apryl. I wanted to win her heart and her body. I wanted to watch her belly round with a child–like Angel's belly rounded. And that would never happen if I made Apryl angry. Angel told Tor that an angry woman does not want sex.

No, I had to say the right words when I approached Apryl the first time.

"You are right, Fallor. I will wait," I said.

"Wait and watch," Fallor said, nodding toward the fey who were serving.

Our brothers gave closed-mouth smiles to the humans and received uncertain smiles in return. Emily said it would take time for humans to see us as something other than killers. I didn't understand how they saw us as killers when their own kind was quick to hurt each other. We removed the heads of the infected to protect the humans that remained, not because we enjoyed killing.

The humans struggled to see the difference. Truthfully, the humans struggled to see many things, and I was not the only fey waiting for an opportunity to speak with a female.

June said we needed to know a female's mind before we could win a female's heart and touch her body. So I knew I couldn't tell Apryl that I wished to touch her soft curves and gently lick her pussy while she slept. She wouldn't like that. My words needed to be about her mind.

I thought back to the questions Emily approved for the dinner dates. We were supposed to ask the females about what they liked. Colors. Foods. Clothes. Weather. Things like that.

Sighing, I uncrossed my arms and studied all the humans who passed through the line. A small female child hugged her mother's leg as they neared the serving tables. I recognized the pair and glanced at Noru. His gaze darted to Abi and Greyly, and his hand dipped to the doll sticking from the waist of his pants.

He hadn't spoken to the child's mother the previous day, but I knew he hoped to speak with her today. When they reached him, Greyly, the tiny female, lifted her plate high, and Abi smiled. It wasn't uncertain.

"Did you bring your baby?" Greyly asked Noru.

He tore his gaze from Abi and gazed at the child.

"I did. Will you show me how to care for her again?" he asked.

The little girl nodded, and Abi set a hand on the child's head while she held out her plate. He gave them each a roll and watched them walk away.

"He is smart," Fallor said. "He lets her come to him."

I glanced at Apryl again. She inched forward with the line, a step at a time, and huddled within her jacket. She was closer to the serving tables now. Closer to me. Rather than wait there for her, I went inside the shed.

"I will take your place," I said when I reached Noru.

"Thank you." He stepped away from his position and strode across the space to where Greyly and Abi ate.

I focused on the next person and deposited a roll on his plate.

He mumbled his thanks for the food and hurried away to

claim a seat. I picked up the next roll and repeated the process, trying not to look down the line to where Apryl waited. Angel said that women could sense desperation, and it turned them off. Yet, I was desperate and craved the day a woman walked up to me and spoke first.

Anticipation filled me as Apryl neared. I wanted to see her pretty brown eyes and full lips curving in a smile for me as Abi's had for Noru. However, Apryl didn't look up when she accepted her bowl.

This was it. This was my chance. I handed Sam her roll and watched Apryl move into position before me.

"Do you like rolls?" I asked, holding out the soft circle of bread.

"Yeah. Thanks," she said, reaching for it.

My fingers brushed her soft palm as I placed the food in her outstretched hand.

"Thanks," she said again. Then, she turned away to hurry after Sam.

I stared after her for a moment and fought not to smile. She hadn't cringed away from my touch and had thanked me twice.

Before the moon rose, I promised myself.

CHAPTER THREE

APRYL

STEW FOR TWO DAYS IN A ROW. REAL CHUNKS OF MEAT AND vegetables sat in my bowl, not the watered-down version we had at my house. I took a bite and closed my eyes in a state of bliss. If the scent of it had made my mouth water, the taste nearly did me in.

Chewing slowly, I savored the meat then opened my eyes to go for the next spoonful. Not being able to clearly see what I spooned up made eating a bit of an adventure. Kind of like eating bridge mix. Sometimes, the piece of chocolate-coated something was good. Sometimes, it was a damn raisin. Not that there was anything raisin-level in my bowl now. The stew was all goodness. It was just the type of goodness that surprised me.

The blurry orange lump on my spoon gave away the carrot before I tasted it. I almost hummed in satisfaction. It'd been ages since I'd had a chunk of carrot like that. Definitely before the world collapsed. And I was pretty sure I hadn't savored it then.

Things changed. Sometimes too fast to keep up with it. Like how I'd bailed on Sam, choosing the first empty seat I'd spotted instead of following her. She didn't seem too upset by it. I could hear her chatting and laughing just a table over. I'd probably just played right into my shy label.

The man next to me started wiping out his bowl— hopefully with his rolls and not his fingers.

"Are you going to eat that?" he asked out of the blue.

"Yes," I said without looking at him. It didn't matter if he was pointing at my bread or my stew. I planned to eat it all.

"Just figured I'd ask since you're eating so slow. Thought you might be getting full."

I'd only taken two bites. He knew darn well I wasn't full.

Ignoring him, I took another bite of stew and kept my roll tucked close to my bowl.

He got the hint and left. Unfortunately, another guy took his place. This one wolfed down his food with a few grunts and didn't ask about mine. When he left and another person claimed that seat, I knew I was taking too long and hurried to keep up with my new companion.

I scraped the bottom of my bowl at the same time they did then waited until they stood to follow them to the dish return and the exit. Following someone was the best way to ensure I didn't run into anything as I left the shed.

Although things were blurry, I could see colors. That's how I knew what was road and what was yard as I walked the neighborhood. And keeping my eyes on the ground in front of me made me less approachable for conversation if anyone was nearby.

I knew Tenacity pretty well by now to recognize the house colors on any given street. The yellow door on the blue and white house I currently called home served as a beacon to guide me down the unshoveled walk. Several sets of footprints marred the white snow.

Veering toward the garage door, I let myself in and found

the shovel. Clearing the walk wasn't exactly helpful, but it was something I could manage...if I took my time. After I'd accidentally torn off the little metal strip from the spare plastic shovel on a crack in the cement, I'd learned not to rush.

My hands were numb by the time I finished and let myself inside. I heard movement in the kitchen and hurried to my room, only a few feet inside the front door. Less conversation was better at this point. I'd probably only annoy whoever was home by either outright not helping or by trying to help and messing up.

Slipping out of my boots and inadequate coat, I hung it on the back of the chair and sat on my twin bed. The room didn't have much in it. The dresser held two t-shirts, two pairs of jeans, a spare set of socks—those were in high demand—and three very frayed and unattractive pairs of thigh-cut underwear that liked to crawl up my ass.

It felt like a lifetime ago that I'd had a walk-in closet full of pretty clothes. Dresses. Underwear that fit. Nice things a girl might take for granted...

Sighing, I lay back and settled in for a long wait until my watered-down portion of dinner.

"Was that Apryl? Did she go straight to her room again?" I heard Michelle ask from the kitchen.

"Yep," Doug, her husband, said. "You told her she can't stay here, right?"

Did they think I'd closed my door?

"I did," Michelle answered. "But maybe we should reconsider. Matt's going to make everyone go on supply runs, and she doesn't cause any trouble. We could do worse."

"She wrecks stuff, Michelle. I don't like kicking her out, but we need to preserve what we have."

A tight ball formed in my chest because he wasn't wrong. I'd tried to help more in the beginning and had caused so much damage. The worst was when I'd burned myself and the food, trying to make dinner. That was the last time they'd let me cook. The runner-up to that was the time I'd tripped over the vacuum cord, trying to clean. I'd broken the vacuum and almost lost a leg. Not really, but it had felt like it.

"Besides," Doug continued. "Preston and I already found two people willing to share her room. The man is used to going out on supply runs and has experience gathering wood. His grandmother helped do whatever was needed around the house."

"Two capable bodies in the place of one? When do they want to move in?" Michelle asked, at least having the decency to sound troubled about it.

"They understand we're giving Apryl a few days to find somewhere else. I'm hoping she doesn't take that long, though. Folks are going out of their way to talk to the supply-run regulars. I heard some outrageous offers were being made. So far, none of them are being swayed by those promises, but I don't want to lose out. Bram and his grandmother are as level-headed as they come."

They already had people lined up? I rolled onto my side and blinked until the urge to cry passed. Tears wouldn't do me any good. Figuring out where to live would. I'd thought I had more time. Today to brainstorm. Tomorrow to research. Then find somewhere before the end of the week. Obviously, people were committing a lot faster than I'd anticipated.

Getting up, I dressed again and slipped out the front door. I wanted to kick myself for not sitting with Sam earlier. She would have been my best resource for finding out if any other fey-human couples were willing to sponsor a human. Without time to come up with a useful skill to contribute to a household here, sponsoring was likely the only solution that would work. Well, one that might work.

The fey didn't hide the fact that they wanted sex and a lot of it. And If I were a human woman newly coupled with one of the fey, I wasn't sure I'd want a third wheel around to witness any of that.

Besides, no one wanted a freeloader. Not even a new couple.

Where did that leave me then? Even if I went to Matt and admitted I couldn't see, he wasn't in charge of the housing. He was letting everyone pick for themselves.

I needed to start thinking outside the box. Or with my box.

I hated the idea of pimping myself out, but sex was one thing I could do well, even mostly blind. If I hooked up with a guy and then let Matt know I'd be a liability if I went out, maybe then I wouldn't be assigned a rotation.

"We're looking for one more," someone called to my right.

Breaking my cardinal rule, I lifted my gaze from the ground. The colorful blur in the direction of the shout looked like a house. I couldn't see any movement around it, though.

Who had yelled then?

"We have three openings in my house," someone else called. "Experienced supply runners only, please."

Several voices overlapped after that. Crap. Was there a meeting in someone's backyard?

I looked down at my feet again and debated fumbling my way over there. If I went slow, I'd be fine. Probably.

Turning, I walked until the blacktop ended and the white began. Transitions were tricky. I lifted my foot and stepped down cautiously, unsure if there was a curb. Subconsciously, I must have expected one because I stumbled when my foot went down past where a curb would have been.

"Careful." A big hand that matched the manly voice closed over my arm and steadied me.

"Thanks," I said, shrugging out of his hold without looking up.

I didn't offer any excuse. That would be an opening for conversation that I didn't want.

Wait. No. I did want conversation.

Rather than continuing forward, I paused and angled my body toward the guy without looking at him.

"Sounds like a big meeting. When did it start?" I asked.

"After the food ran out. Are you looking for a new place to live too?"

"Maybe," I said, pretending to study the house. "Depends on the accommodations. Is there an open room at your place?"

"Yes," he said, sounding a mix of hesitant and surprised.

"Are you looking for someone specific, like an experienced supply runner?"

"No. Nothing specific."

My pulse started to pound with excitement. "That's great. I haven't gone out yet, myself. But if there's an open spot at your place, I'll take it. Do you need to talk this over with anyone?" I turned my head away from him as if looking down the street for someone else.

"No."

"Okay," I said, trying to keep my cool. "How soon can I move in?"

"Now?"

I couldn't believe my luck. No skill required, and I hadn't even needed to offer sex. Trying to keep my composure, I nodded.

"Great. I'll go pack up my things and let my housemates know. Would you mind meeting back here in an hour?" It wouldn't take me long to pack, but I wasn't sure if anyone was home to tell.

"I don't mind. Take your time. I'll be here waiting."

He sounded so nice. I desperately needed nice. And patient. And understanding.

Watching my feet, I hurried away down the street. Nerves and fear had butterflies dancing in my stomach. I had another house, but for how long? I needed to figure out a way to be useful right from the start. Possibilities turned over in my mind as I walked.

CHAPTER FOUR

SCATH

UNABLE TO BELIEVE WHAT HAD JUST HAPPENED, I WATCHED APRYL calmly walk away. She'd agreed to live with me. Me. I struggled not to smile. Or follow her. I really wanted to do both.

When I'd spotted her walking down the street, I'd told myself I would say hello and nothing else. But then she'd stumbled before I could. I'd moved quickly to steady her, not thinking how she might react, only worried she would hurt herself. The way she'd pulled away from my touch had pierced a hole in my chest. But then she'd started speaking to me.

She'd asked to live with *me*. Scath.

I was the luckiest fey alive.

The conversation played through my mind again, and her carefully worded "Depends on the accommodations" stood out. I needed to go home and ensure everything was clean, just like Mom taught us. And food. I should have food out. I saw how hungry Apryl was this morning.

Turning away from her retreating form, I started jogging for the wall.

"Scath," Fallor called. "Where are you going?"

"Home. I will be back."

He caught up to me and cleared the wall at the same time I did.

"I will go with you."

I grinned.

"You hope to see Emily."

"I wish to know what you are doing. Emily said we cannot give them extra food during this time of transition. I don't want you undermining her efforts."

"I understand her efforts and will do nothing to undermine them and risk our brothers' future chances at females of their own."

"You say that as if you already have a female."

I flashed him a smile.

"I do. Apryl asked to live with me."

Fallor made a sound of disbelief.

"I understand your doubt. I doubted it too. She truly wishes to live with me, but it will depend on the accommodations. I will clean my house and return for her in an hour."

"I'll help and return with you." More than doubt laced his tone.

"Speak your thoughts," I said.

"Hannah said many things she did not mean."

"You think Apryl lied?"

Fallor shrugged.

"I will wait with you so you are not alone."

Fallor was a good friend, but he was wrong. Apryl would be there. I saw the excitement on her face before she looked away. She wished to live with me. Didn't she?

I thought of Hannah and how she'd let Shax believe she cared for him when she did not. She only wanted the supplies he provided. Did I care if that was why Apryl wished to live with me? For food? No. That is why Angel started talking to Shax, and she eventually gave him her heart.

Unbothered by Apryl's motivations, I decided my goals hadn't changed. I would get her to look at me before the moon rose. Even if Apryl only wanted my home and food, I would find ways to know her mind and then win her heart. After that, she would let me taste her body, and I would see our baby grow inside of her.

Satisfied with my plan, I ran faster and cleared Tolerance's wall a few minutes later. Fallor followed me to the house I claimed as my own. It was large compared to my hut in Ernisi but much smaller than most of the surrounding homes with two levels. It had a large front porch with a rocking chair that James said was meant for sitting and watching people and sipping sweet tea. Inside, only one of the three bedrooms had a bed. But the living room had a comfortable sofa, and the kitchen was full of cooking implements and food.

Fallor vacuumed the entire house while I started a mid-day meal from one of the boxes in the cabinet. Emily had explained how to prepare these meals. Brown the meat. Add the packet and the water. Then add the noodles and cook. They were easy and filling, and humans loved them.

I selected a can of vegetables and opened it but didn't add it to the pan.

"Should I make her one of the chocolate boxes?" I asked Fallor.

He shut off the vacuum and put it away in the closet.

"Do you know how?" he asked.

"No."

"Then let her make it when she arrives. Human females love to cook."

"Brooke does not. Hannah does not."

"Fine. If Apryl does not like to cook, she can read the box for you, and you can cook for her. Why waste food if she is not hungry for it?"

I grunted in acknowledgment and closed the cupboard door.

As soon as the meal was complete, I turned off the stove and covered it. Then I looked around, considering the house. While I'd wanted a female of my own, I hadn't thought it would happen so quickly. I had very little to offer her. Many of the houses were filled with furniture. My house was mostly empty, and I feared she would reject it as soon as she stepped inside.

"Humans are used to having more than this. Emily's home has three chairs, a big couch, a tiny couch, a table in the middle, a plant, lamps—"

Fallor came over and clapped a hand on my shoulder.

"Do not worry about things that haven't yet happened. When Apryl arrives, you will ask her what she would like in her new home. Then we will find it for her. First, we need to ensure she wants to live here."

Thankful that he didn't voice his doubt again, I nodded and strode for the door where I paused and inhaled deeply. The house smelled like food. Hopefully, Apryl would find it a welcome scent, and it would entice her to stay.

"Do you truly believe she won't be there?" I asked.

"I hope she is. Every female who accepts one of my brothers prods another female to make the same choice."

"And once we are all claimed by females, then Emily will focus on you?" I asked with a grin.

Fallor grunted and jumped over the wall. I hurried after him.

"What if Emily secretly wants one of the human men, like

Garrett or Ryan? What will you do then?" I asked as we started running.

"Gather supplies for them and protect their babies when they are born."

I nodded, understanding what he wasn't saying. Emily would be his even if she wasn't. That was how Tor felt about June when she was Adam's. June cried many tears when Adam released her. For Fallor's sake, I hoped that Emily's heart wasn't already taken.

"Once I win Apryl's heart, I will help you win Emily's," I said.

Fallor shook his head at me.

"You do not believe me? Look at how quickly Apryl agreed to live with me. Emily will do the same."

"Focus on your female. Mya says that if something seems too good to be true, then it probably is."

"Yet, she is growing Drav's baby inside of her. Is that not too good to be true?" I scoffed. "Mom says Mya is trying to protect our hearts. My heart is fine."

"Will it be fine if Apryl does not meet you, though?"

I laughed away his concern but felt the pain it caused. Apryl would be there. She had to be. She said she would.

The human guards on Tenacity's wall noted our arrival with a glance but didn't yell or spit at us. I would miss their old ways of greeting us, but June and Matt also warned all of Tenacity that fey mistreatment wouldn't be tolerated any more than human mistreatment.

We knew spit wasn't mistreatment, though. Drav shared how Mya kissed his cock so deeply that he felt her spit-coated tongue slide against the underside of his shaft. No fey would be foolish enough to discourage a female from sharing her spit even if she meant it for our faces. We knew where she longed to spit.

I was glad the males no longer spit, though, or Angel would have had to explain to them that they were showing their desperation. Although the men pretended otherwise, they understood they were losing their females, one at a time, to us.

When Apryl left with me today, perhaps Abi would hear of her wise choice and leave with Greyly after that. And then that other female with skin darker than Apryl, who Eitri watched, might leave as well.

All Apryl needed to do was look into my eyes and tell me to take her to her new home.

My happiness faded when we arrived at the same spot and Apryl wasn't there. Fallor didn't say anything. He didn't need to. I felt his doubt.

"I think we arrived early. We should wait."

Voices drifted from the other side of the house. Humans speaking about living arrangements. What if Apryl was there, looking for a human home?

"I'll be right back," I said to Fallor.

He grunted and crossed his arms, settling in to wait.

CHAPTER FIVE

APRYL

NERVOUS DIDN'T BEGIN TO COVER HOW I FELT AS I WALKED DOWN the street while carrying my small bag of clothes. Fighting the urge to cry, I kept my head down and eyes on the road. I shouldn't have waited around at the house for someone to show up. Because I had, I was running late.

Now, fear-fueled questions bounced around in my head. What if he wasn't there? I hadn't asked his name or his house number and had no idea how to find him. I could ask around. But I had nothing to go off of. No description other than he'd had a big hand and a deep voice.

I tried to tell myself not to worry. He'd been quick to offer. That meant he was serious, right? And if he was serious, he'd wait for me.

But what if he wasn't serious? What if it had been a prank and I'd just given up my spot?

I tried to breathe through my fear and tell myself that was nonsense, but the feeling wouldn't let go. So much was riding on this. Why hadn't I asked him his name? How could I be so stupid?

For the millionth time, I wished I'd simply packed my

bag and left. I could have let everyone know about the change after I made it through the first night. But no, I'd waited like a dumbass until Michelle showed up because I'd wanted to witness her reaction when I told her they could give my room to the people they had waiting. Some part of me had wanted to hear just a smidge of concern or remorse. I was an idiot. There hadn't been any. Michelle had been audibly relieved that I'd found a place and wouldn't be coming back.

I hit the end of the block and turned onto the final road. The urge to look up and scan for him tugged at me. But that would be pointless since one blur could look like the next at this distance. So I kept walking, placing one foot in front of the other.

When the low murmur of voices reached my ears, my steps slowed, and I risked lifting my gaze just a little. A tannish blur moved in the center of the road.

I breathed a sigh of relief and headed toward him.

"Have you been waiting long?" I asked.

"No."

He sounded a little different, but maybe he was annoyed I was late.

"Sorry I'm late. I had to wait for one of my housemates to show up so I could let them know I wasn't coming back."

"I understand."

But he didn't exactly sound understanding or concerned like he had when I'd spoken to him before. He sounded uncomfortable now.

"Is everything okay?" I asked.

"Are you certain you wish to leave your current home?"

Panic knifed through me. I was losing him. How? Why? Had he found someone else while I was gone?

I needed to fix this and only had one ace card up my sleeve.

Mentally preparing myself, I jumped off the desperation cliff with arms wide open.

"I'm certain," I said breathlessly.

I closed the distance between us, and he uncrossed his arms, an obvious invitation. Swallowing hard and knowing I needed to seal the deal, I closed my eyes, stood on my toes, and brushed my lips against his.

Only, I didn't quite make it. He was taller than I'd realized, and my mouth only grazed his chin.

"Sorry," I whispered, mortified that I'd missed.

He didn't help me out by bending down even a little, though. Obviously, he wanted to show me I'd need to work for my place. Okay. Fine. I'd suspected the quick invitation would have some catches. Understanding didn't stop my face from heating as I looped my hands around his neck for an assist. I reached his lips on my second attempt. And for half a second, it wasn't horrible. His lips were warm and soft under mine before they firmed, and he turned his head.

"Not into public displays?" I asked. "That's fine. We can take this back to your place, and we can do more there."

"I don't understand," he said. "Do what?"

Asking me to say exactly what I was offering was a smart move on his part. If I didn't offer what he wanted, he could walk away right now, which wasn't something I could afford.

"Anything you want. Kissing. A blow job. Sex. It's yours."

I jumped at the sound of a growl behind me.

The man in front of me set his hands on my shoulders and slowly eased me away from him.

"Thank you for the offer, Apryl, but I am not interested in your kisses or pussy."

My brain glitched at the use of that word. Normal people didn't use it in conversation like he just did. Normal human people, anyway.

But other people did.

I lifted my head and stared at the grey blur-blob that was the man's head and internally swore.

Oh my god, I kissed a fey.

No, I'd done way more than that. I'd propositioned him.

My thoughts had another hiccup when I realized he'd turned me down. A fey had turned *me* down. They never turned any female down. They were desperate for women. Any shape, color, or size. They didn't care. Except for me, apparently. Sam had said they were watching me. Did that mean they knew I couldn't see shit? Was I a reject? The first rejected female ever?

Worse than that was the realization that I hadn't been offered a place in some other house here in Tenacity. A fey had offered to take me in. And now he'd changed his mind? He couldn't. I had nowhere else to go now. I'd given up my house.

The tears I'd been trying to hold back for the last hour welled up.

"Please," I whispered brokenly as the first tear fell. "If you don't want any sexual favors, that's fine. Just tell me what you do want."

Another growl rumbled behind me, reminding me that we weren't alone. Just how many of his friends had witnessed my spectacle?

The fey holding my arms abruptly released me, and I sniffled.

"I don't have anywhere else to go," I said.

"Live with me, Apryl," another fey said harshly from behind me.

Wiping at my face, I ducked my head and partially turned toward him.

"Okay. What do you want?" I asked.

He growled again.

"Nothing."

He sounded completely angry when he said it, and I didn't blame him. He obviously didn't want me living with him, but the fey had soft hearts when it came to females. Well, they usually did.

I regretted that the concerned one hadn't wanted to take me in. Actually, I mourned the whole situation. I'd thought I'd said yes to a human housing arrangement, not a fey one. But maybe this was better. I'd heard that the women who housed with the fey didn't have to go on supply runs. They didn't have to do anything but spread their legs. But this one wasn't asking for that. Why exactly did he want to host me?

"Okay," I murmured. "If you change your mind, just let me know. I'm willing to do whatever for a warm bed and some food."

He growled again and said something that sounded like, "I was a fool."

"Why do you have nowhere to go?" the first fey asked. "Matt said there were enough houses for everyone to have a place to sleep at night."

"I had one," I said. "But now that everyone can choose who they want to live with, my housemates asked me to leave. I've been having a hard time finding someone else to take me in. Everyone is looking for people who have useful skills. Like experience going out for wood or supplies." I gave a woeful shrug. "I don't have those skills."

"We can speak to Matt, and he will help you find somewhere else to live," the first fey said. "You will not be forced to live somewhere you do not want to live."

The tears fell a little faster as I realized why he was saying that. The other fey didn't want me to live with him either. Knowing how the fey wanted to protect all women, the second fey had likely only offered because I'd said I had nowhere else. It sucked being the reject.

"Matt's not really in a position to help me. If he tried forcing someone to take me in after telling everyone they had a choice, people would go crazy. And it's okay if neither of you wants to house me. I understand that having someone underfoot who you aren't interested in would probably send the wrong message to any woman you might be interested in. Do you know of any fey who might be?"

I knew I sounded desperate, but I didn't care. The sun was high, and I needed to figure out where I'd be sleeping before it set.

"You will stay with me, Apryl," the second fey repeated, sounding a bit resigned.

"I don't want to mess up your chances with a girl you might actually want."

Fingers brushed the underside of my chin, nudging it up. I closed my eyes so the second fey wouldn't see my unfocused gaze as he turned my face toward his.

The long moment of silence that followed worried me.

"You won't mess up anything," he finally said quietly.

I almost felt bad for him. I messed up a lot. No doubt about that. How long would it take before he passed me off to someone else? How long before everyone knew I was deadweight? If one of them would just take me up on my blow job offer, I was sure I could at least be useful that way.

"All right," I said. "If you're willing to take me in, I'm all yours."

"My name is Scath," he said, his light touch brushing over my chin.

"Scath," I repeated. "It's nice to meet you."

His thumb brushed over my skin again. It almost felt like a caress.

"Are you afraid?" he asked.

"No. Should I be?"

"No." He released my chin. I ducked my head and opened my eyes again, nodding toward the other fey. "And what's your name?" I asked.

"Fallor."

"I'm sorry things didn't work out between us, Fallor."

CHAPTER SIX

SCATH

FALLOR GRUNTED AND GLANCED AT ME. I STARED AT THE TOP OF Apryl's knit cap.

How had everything gone so wrong? She'd agreed to live with me. Then she saw Fallor and kissed him. When he hadn't returned her affection, she'd looked up at him and shed tears in her grief.

It was just like June and Adam. I thought I would only need to figure out a way to win her heart, but she refused to look at me. If it wasn't fear, then what else could it be?

"Do I still need to ask for permission to live with you?" Apryl asked. "I remember the speech Mya gave a few weeks back when we were living in Tolerance."

There had been so many females within the walls at that time. I wished I would have noticed her then. If she had seen my face first, would she have given me her kisses?

"No," Fallor said. "We can choose who lives with us. But Mya will remove any females who do not have good intentions."

"Okay," Apryl said, hugging her bag to her chest.

She looked so lost and helpless, and I hated it. I wanted her in my home and in my bed, but not because she felt she had no other choice. And not when she was still yearning for Fallor.

I rubbed a hand over the back of my neck, frustrated.

"Can Scath carry you?" Fallor asked, giving me a hard look.

Right. He didn't want to carry her even if she did seem to prefer his arms.

"Yes. Of course," Apryl said.

She stepped closer to me, still not looking up at me, and I reminded myself to have patience. Fallor had been right. Her willingness had been too good to be true. But that didn't mean I couldn't still win her heart.

I lifted her into my arms and looked down at her face. She'd closed her eyes again.

"It's a very pretty sky today," I said. "Don't you think so, Apryl?"

"Uh, yeah. It's pretty," she said without opening her eyes.

Before I could be disappointed, she rested her head against my chest. My heart swelled at the contact, and I shifted her weight to press her closer.

"Am I too heavy?" she asked.

"No," I said, starting to walk. I could have held her for days and not grown tired. Definitely hard, but not tired.

Fallor kept pace with me, his gaze flicking between me and Apryl. I knew he had no interest in her but still wished he would go follow Emily for a while. His face would only remind Apryl of her desire for him. Before I could find a reason to send him away, Matt called out to us.

"What's going on?" he said, gesturing to Apryl.

"Apryl is going to live with me," I said.

"Apryl?" Matt asked when she didn't look up at him.

"Yeah?" she said, turning her face to rub her cheek against me.

"Are you leaving of your own free will?"

"Yes. I am."

Fallor and I exchanged a look. It would be right to tell Matt that people were being kicked out of their homes. But if we did, he might find somewhere else for Apryl to stay. And I didn't want that. I also didn't want to prevent any of my brothers from having the same opportunity I had.

"Okay then," Matt said with a nod. "You're in good hands, Apryl. Just don't do anything to cause any trouble over there."

"I understand."

After a nod at us, Matt continued on his way.

"I doubt she is the only one," I said.

Fallor nodded. "I will tell the others what to watch for."

He jogged away as Apryl shifted in my arms. Need pounded through me at the feel of her hands sliding up my chest. She was touching me. Willingly. I swallowed and tried to think of something clever to say to show my appreciation for her mind.

"You don't need to look for other females. I meant what I said. Blow jobs. Sex. Whatever you want," she said. "I'm good with my mouth. I promise."

My balls tingled and my shaft hardened at the same time my heart shriveled. Her touches weren't real. She still thought she had to offer her body.

"I will not use your body in exchange for living with me," I said, moving again.

She slowly withdrew her hands, and I struggled to come up with something to say as she exhaled heavily. Emily said we should ask females about their interests.

"Do you like to cook?" I asked.

"Uh, not really. I tend to burn things."

"Oh. What do you like to do?"

Her breathing sped up. "Nothing," she whispered.

I grunted, unsure how I was supposed to know her mind if she didn't like to do anything. Perhaps she didn't know what she liked doing because she hadn't tried many things. I imagined bringing her to the melted dicks where the other women met for feight club. Apryl would be fierce and beautiful, shooting Angel's bow. Or if she didn't like that, she could go to Emily's knitting circle. Or maybe Brooke's sketch classes. My cock throbbed at the thought of being her model. Brooke loved staring at Solin's cock. He has many sketches of it from her.

I would find something Apryl liked doing, and we would talk about that.

Liking my plan, I looked down at her. She shook in my arms.

"Are you warm enough?" I asked.

"Yes."

I frowned, noting the way she continued to shake. Why did she not want to tell me she was cold? I considered her thin jacket as I approached the wall.

"It will feel colder when I run," I said. "Hide your face against me, and tell me if I need to stop to warm you."

"You won't need to. I'll be fine," she said, turning her face toward me.

My frown deepened. Mom had said that fine doesn't always mean fine. This felt like one of those situations.

Perhaps once Apryl saw the meal I had waiting for her, she would feel better. Food always made Angel happier.

Deciding that was a good plan, I jumped over the wall and started to run.

Apryl buried her face against me and shook harder. I held her close to share my warmth, and my concern changed into confusion. She didn't feel cold. Why would she shake like that then? I considered all the stories I'd heard regarding a female shaking, and the one that stood out most vividly was Hannah's nightmares. Merdon said she trembled for a long time afterward out of fear and regret.

Apryl said she wasn't afraid. What would she regret so badly that it made her shake? Agreeing to live with me? That didn't make sense after she'd offered to welcome my cock into her mouth and pussy. But what if she'd changed her mind?

I ran faster, desperate to reach Tolerance before she asked me to return her. If I could just show her the food I had, not only the cooked meal but everything in the cupboards, then perhaps she would be willing to stay for a while. Long enough to convince her that I would be a good male for her.

The sight of the distant wall fueled my speed, and I cleared it with ease but didn't stop to put her down. She didn't look up. She did nothing but tremble in my arms.

Some of my brothers paused to watch me pass, their eyes on Apryl. It was good I'd made it this far with her. If she didn't like my food or my house, then maybe she would give another one of my brothers a chance.

An image flashed in my head of Apryl standing on her toes and pulling Fallor down for a kiss. My insides gave a tight squeeze that I couldn't ignore, and I acknowledged that I didn't want her to choose one of my brothers. I wanted her to choose me.

She finally lifted her head from my chest when I stopped in front of the door. However, rather than looking at her new home, she played with the strap of her bag, showing no interest in where we were.

Reluctantly, I set her down and reached around her to open the door.

"Go inside," I encouraged. "Look around."

She ducked her head, staring at the floor as she slowly entered. I waited for her reaction, but she never lifted her gaze.

CHAPTER SEVEN

APRYL

HAVING NEVER TRAVELED BY FEY BEFORE, I HADN'T EXPECTED THE gentle way Scath had carried me. Or how good it had felt to have his arms wrapped around me. Since the quakes, people focused on survival, not hugs. But, damn, I'd missed hugs, and that was exactly what it had felt like in his arms. Like he'd been hugging me the whole way…right until he put me down in front of the blurry, gaping maw of his open front door.

"Go inside," he said. "Look around."

The absurdity of his polite invitation made me want to snort. Navigating unfamiliar spaces was pure hell. Coffee tables, rugs, and so many other things presented trip hazards. If I were alone, I'd take my time and explore the space slowly, counting steps and studying the differently colored and shaped blobs. But I couldn't do that with Scath right behind me, not if I didn't want him to know I couldn't see.

I needed to walk my ass into his house like it was no big deal. Then I'd figure out a way to impress the hell out of him so any other women Fallor found wouldn't even tempt Scath. I couldn't afford to be rejected again. Who knew how many chances like this I'd get?

Keeping my eyes on the tannish blur beneath my feet, I cautiously advanced a few feet and listened to my footsteps faintly echo. Carpet muted footsteps while tile and wood enhanced them. And harder surfaces meant rugs. Crap.

As I was worrying about tripping on something I wouldn't see, I caught the scent of food and paused. It smelled like meat. I inhaled deeply.

"Are you hungry?" Scath asked.

The questions he'd asked on the way over and the utter hopeless defeat I'd felt answering them hit me all over again. And I had to remind myself that he hadn't immediately turned around and returned me to Tenacity when I'd admitted I couldn't cook or do anything helpful. That had to mean something. Right?

I still couldn't bring myself to gobble down his food the moment I walked in his door though. I needed to do something first. Anything.

"I'm fine, thank you," I said, unable to accept his food first thing. It was bad enough I knew that I was a resource leech. I didn't want him to know that right off. "Can you show me to the bedroom I'll be using?"

"Yes. It's this way." He led the way down the hall and stepped into a bedroom.

Under a set of windows, a large, multi-colored square took up the middle of the room. A bed. A dark spot on each side probably meant nightstands too. I turned my head, scanning for less obvious color differences that would represent other furniture but didn't spot any, which made me nervous.

I moved forward slowly, moving my head like I was taking in the room at the same time. Pretending to test the softness of the mattress, I set my hand on the bed and walked around it. Nothing got in the way of my progress until the nightstand.

"I will find a dresser for you," he said when I set my bag on the bed.

"Is there a closet?" I asked.

"Yes. Here." He went to one of the doors and opened it, turning on a light.

I joined him in the spacious walk-in. Shadows marked the back of deep shelves, and tan lines represented the hanging rods. A few colored blobs interrupted the otherwise off-whiteness, indicating there might be some clothes already hung. But until I explored a little on my own, I wouldn't know for sure.

"If you don't mind me putting my things here, there's no need for a dresser," I said.

"I don't mind," he said.

"Thanks."

"I've never had a human here before," he said. "If there's anything missing, will you tell me?"

"Of course," I said, feeling down over his desire to improve his house for whoever Fallor might find.

Then, I realized he'd just given me a way to be useful. Actually, I had several ways to be useful now. Emily had said those dinner dates were to hone the feys' conversational skills, even though we all knew it was really an opportunity for the fey to hook up with a human. But, considering how awkward some of the fey were, maybe Scath would like a chance to practice his conversation skills on me despite his lack of interest in me.

"Your home seems very nice, and you've obviously put some effort into it. I can smell the soap. It must be frustrating having this ready and waiting only for women to generally ignore you."

"We understand females are unsure of us. Emily says most

fear our size and strength and that we should use questions to help start positive conversations."

"What kinds of questions?"

"Come. We can talk while we eat lunch."

I nodded this time, more at ease with eating his food now that I knew I had a way to be useful, and followed him from the bedroom.

"Emily said that we should ask questions to get to know a female's mind," he said. "I've tried, but females don't like answering direct questions. They walk away."

"Okay. What are some of the questions you've asked?"

"What is your favorite food?"

"That's a good one."

He grunted then stopped walking. I blinked and glanced at the blobs around us, realizing I'd followed him into the kitchen. The black blur interrupting the stretch of grey was probably the stove.

Dishes clinked as he took down plates from a cupboard.

"What is your favorite food?" he asked, and I knew, this time, he was asking me.

"Oh, um. I guess any food is my favorite food at this point."

"Yes. My brothers and I hear that answer often, which tells us nothing of the female's mind and makes the question a bad choice."

"Ah. I see. What if you phrased it differently? Like, 'If you could have any food you wanted, what food would you choose?'"

"That is a good question," he said. "How would you answer it?"

"Right now? I'd say whatever it is I'm smelling." I inhaled deeply. "It smells amazing."

"It is a box meal. Emily said humans like them. It has meat and noodles. I did not add vegetables."

The way he said that last part, like it was some kind of dark warning he thought I wasn't going to respond to well to, had me grinning a little.

"I hear fey don't like many vegetables. Is that true?"

"We like meats and will eat some vegetables."

"What's your favorite kind?" I asked, trailing behind him when he started walking again.

"Not these little green balls."

I chuckled. "Peas? They're harmless and filled with so many vitamins and nutrients. They're good for you."

"You can eat them all," he said.

I heard the clink of plates and saw the fuzzy shape of the table. Feeling my way to a chair while his back was turned, I sat and waited for him to join me.

"What other questions do you have?" I asked as I slowly felt for a utensil.

"Here," Scath said, taking my hand and setting it on the fork.

My pulse leapt and ignited an explosion of panic that heated my face.

"Emily said to ask females about their favorite color, but Bauts said his female left dinner early when he asked that," he said as if he hadn't just helped me find my fork.

"Anyone who signs up for those dinner dates knows it's not just for conversation practice," I said, pretending like what he'd done was no big deal. "She probably got spooked when he started asking about favorites. Sometimes it's easier to offer information about yourself and then turn the conversation to your companion. For example, this tastes like ground beef. My grandma used to make these amazing homemade meatballs in gravy that my brother and I would fight over. She made them every holiday without fail. I miss those meatballs. Are there any foods you miss?"

Stuffing a bite into my mouth, I listened to his grunt and tried to breathe through my lingering panic.

"I haven't tried a meatball. If you tell me how to make them, I can cook them for you."

"Oh, no. That's okay," I said after swallowing my bite. "I don't expect you to cook for me."

"Why not? You do not like cooking and I do." He said it so frankly and without a hint of judgment or annoyance that I believed he really didn't see a problem with it just like he hadn't apparently seen anything wrong with the fact I hadn't used my eyes to find my fork. Plus, he'd said he'd never had a meatball. I'd be doing him a favor, then, right?

"Okay. Sure. Next time you find some ground beef, we'll give it a try." I took another bite.

"We can make them for dinner," he said. "What other questions should I ask?"

Stunned that he had more beef, I swallowed hard and considered what it would mean to eat two meat-heavy meals in one day. That was crazy talk.

"Maybe we should ration the meat a little and wait until tomorrow."

"The freezer in the garage is full of meat. There's no need to ration."

"A freezer full?"

"Yes."

"Just how much food do you have?"

He left the table, and I heard cupboards opening.

"This much. But I can get more."

I lifted my gaze from my plate and looked at the patchwork of colors in the kitchen that had previously been a wash of white. We'd known that the fey were keeping the majority of the supplies gathered on the supply runs, but I didn't think anyone realized what that meant. While we'd lived in Tolerance, things had been almost as lean as they were now in Tenacity, which was why people had ransacked their supply shed.

"That's a lot," I said, quietly.

And I wasn't sure what I felt about it. Part of me thought it was shitty that the supplies weren't being more equally divided, but that was the part of me that was frustrated with my inability to survive on my own. If I were the one leaving for supplies, would I still think it should be equally divided while other people stayed behind and did nothing? Probably not.

Scath's shadowy shape moved.

"Do you like chocolate?" he asked.

"Yes."

"I have a box that will make a chocolate cake. I will make it for us but need help reading the directions. Will you read it for me?"

He came over to the table and handed me the box.

Without thinking, I brought the packaging almost to my nose to make out what it said. It wasn't chocolate cake. It was brownies. My mouth started to water a second before I became aware of what I was doing and jerked the box away from my face.

"Let's finish eating first," I said, trying to buy myself some time to figure out how to read the box without being obvious about it.

CHAPTER EIGHT

SCATH

HIDING MY DISAPPOINTMENT, I WATCHED APRYL SET THE BOX aside. Mya and the other females here loved chocolate. They obsessed over it and squealed whenever someone returned with more. I'd thought the sweet dessert would be exactly what I needed to win Apryl's interest. If not in me, at least in staying here since she hadn't seemed that impressed when I'd told her about the freezer of meat either. What could I do to show her this was a good home for her? That I was a good male for her?

She picked up her fork and continued eating, slowly scraping her way around her plate. She never looked up at me. Not once.

"Do my eyes scare you?" I asked, needing to know.

"What?" She jerked and looked up at me before quickly looking away. "No. Your eyes don't scare me. But I've heard that some people do find them disturbing. I think that's just because they're still getting used to the differences. When they do, their attitudes will change."

I didn't care about other humans; I cared about Apryl and what Apryl thought of me. But I knew better than to ask if she found me handsome. Brog had tried that during his dinner date, and his female had told him that wasn't an appropriate question for two people getting to know one another. I didn't understand why, though. Angel explained sexual attraction to us. If a female didn't find a male handsome, she would never let him lick her pussy until she screamed.

Sighing softly, I watched Apryl take another bite and wondered if her pussy would taste as good as my brothers said their females' pussies tasted. My cock hardened at the thought, and I shifted in my seat, trying to give it more space.

"Would you like some peas?" I asked, remembering the vegetable just before she finished.

"Sure."

I got up and retrieved the bowl from the counter. It wasn't very warm anymore, but hot or cold, it didn't change the texture or taste. I gave her two generous scoops and watched her use her fork to mash them.

"Do they taste better when they are flat," I asked.

She smiled. It was the prettiest I'd ever seen her, and I promised myself that I would find every way to make her smile more.

"It makes them easier to pick up," she said. "Otherwise, they tend to roll off my fork."

My female was as beautiful as she was smart.

"Would you like more meat noodle mix?" I asked.

"There's more?"

The shock and hope in her tone pleased me. Finally, I had something that interested her.

"Yes."

I retrieved the pan from the stove and scraped what remained onto her plate. She took another bite, mixing her pea paste in with the noodles as I returned the pot to the sink.

"Scath, this is so good. Thank you," she said when I joined

her. "I'm definitely getting the better end of this deal. Do you have any other conversation starters you want to discuss?"

I realized what she was doing.

"You do not owe me conversation for the food," I said.

She stopped eating and turned her head toward me without looking up from her plate.

"I understand that you're not interested in me, but I don't want to be a burden either."

It felt like a hound was attempting to chew its way through my middle. She thought I wasn't interested in her? How? Why? I opened my mouth to clarify but closed it just as quickly. Telling her how much I wanted to taste her lips and hold her would show my desperation, and she would run away.

"You are not a burden, Apryl," I said instead.

She nodded her head slowly. "Okay."

I watched her eat until she sat back with a groan.

"I'll probably be sick from eating so much, but that was too good to stop."

I collected her plate and fork and went to the sink. She remained in her seat and nudged the box mix closer in front of her as I ran the water for dishes. I found it odd how she leaned so close to the box. Was she smelling the mix? It did smell good. Sweet and like chocolate.

While the sink filled, I pulled out a bowl and a flat spoon. The measuring cups were marked with different colored handles. I memorized the colors for the measurements and hoped I would impress Apryl with my ability to tell the difference between the sizes. All the humans knew how to read except for the young ones. Kerr was learning from Cassie in addition to how to doctor humans but didn't have much spare time to teach the rest of us between that and caring for his young.

I hated that I couldn't read and was dependent on Apryl. Hannah told Shax that females liked independent men.

"Emily says that most desserts require water, oil, and eggs," I said. "If you tell me how much of each, I will add it."

Apryl provided the measurements, and I quickly added them before retrieving the box from her to add the powder. As I did, I remembered what step I'd missed.

"I know how to start the oven, but I don't understand the temperatures. I-I need help."

She popped out of her chair.

"I don't mind helping." She shuffled toward the stove and leaned down to inspect the buttons. They were small and confusing, so I understood why she took time before touching one of them.

"There," she said after several adjustments. "It should be preheating. But you might want to check inside of it to make sure no one left any pans in there."

She took several steps back, and I quickly did as she suggested. There was a blackened stone circle inside that I removed and set on the stovetop.

"What is this for?" I asked.

She reached out and touched it, tracing her fingers around its circumference.

"A pizza stone."

"Do you like pizza?" I asked.

"Depends on the kind. I'm not a fan of traditional marinara, but I had this pizza with chicken and barbeque on it that I dream about sometimes. If I let myself think about it too much, I start missing a lot of things that are gone now."

"Tell me what you miss," I said, eager to hear what things I might learn to entice her to stay.

"My cat, Heimdall. I couldn't take him with me when I was evacuated."

"Drav told me he saw pets when he first came here. A dog that wasn't like a hellhound and a cat that hissed at him. We didn't understand how humans would want to keep either creature until Merdon returned with a cat for Hannah. All the females made soft noises at it and wanted to hold it. Except Hannah. She said it would make her eyes water."

"Allergies."

"Yes. Do you have allergies?" I asked.

"No."

"I will find you a cat," I said, pleased I'd found something.

"Thanks, but no. I couldn't imagine trying to take care of a cat during all of this. I'd be too afraid of someone trying to eat it if we ran out of food."

Disappointed that I couldn't get her a cat, I whisked the batter together again and dug out a pan.

"Wait," she said when I would have poured it in. "I think you have to grease the pan first, but I'm not sure that's the right size."

She brought the empty box to her face.

"It says an eight-by-eight." She set the box down and tracked her finger over the edge of the pan like she was measuring it with her fingers instead of her eyes. "I think this is a nine-by-thirteen. Baking it in a larger pan will change the cooking time and make a really thin brownie. Do you have a smaller square pan?"

She may not like cooking, but she knew plenty about it. Appreciative of her knowledge, I traded the large one for a smaller one and listened to her explanation of how to grease a pan.

Once the brownies were in the oven, she set the timer and ran her hand over the counter near the sink.

"I can help wash the dishes if there are no knives in the water," she offered.

"No. I can wash them. Would you like to read? I have books by the couch."

"Books? Why do you have books if you can't read?"

I could feel the tips of my ears heat and knew I couldn't tell her the real reason I'd collected the books with the bare-chested human males on the covers.

Groth had said that Terri would touch Azio when she read the man-chest books and sometimes allowed Azio to lick her pussy while she read. But not in the same room as Groth. It made her uncomfortable being exposed to someone other than Azio.

However, what Groth was able to observe helped us understand there are many different ways to arouse a female. Without the books, Terri liked it when Azio teased her legs with light touches. It could take many long minutes before she led him to the bedroom and shut the door. If she was reading, though, she would tease Azio's ear very briefly before asking if they could go to the bedroom. According to Azio, licking to the side of her clit was her favorite, and circling it worked well to build need. But suckling it when she started moving her hips was a good way to make her gasp and pant.

Azio swore that she wanted more sex and licking on the days she read the man-chest books.

Kerr hadn't learned enough words to read a full book himself, but Drav listened to a book and said they described sex. Angel said that reading sexy descriptions could be a turn-on for a lot of women.

But I couldn't say any of that to Apryl.

"I would like to learn to read. Will you teach me?" I asked instead.

"I'm not a teacher, but I'll help you find someone who is, okay?"

Relieved that she wasn't suspicious, I nodded and asked, "Would you like to watch a movie?"

"Sure, if you pick it out."

I strode toward the living room, eager to get her on the couch. It wasn't a big piece of furniture, and I hoped she would lean against me to get comfortable.

CHAPTER NINE

APRYL

HELPING SCATH MAKE THE BROWNIES HADN'T BEEN AS demoralizing as I'd thought it would be. He hadn't questioned how close I'd held the box to my face or my reluctance to pitch in to do the actual work. He seemed completely content with just instruction and didn't think I was a burden. How did I know? I'd admitted to feeling like I was.

And he'd even been cool about answering. He hadn't tried to reassure me or made promises that would have been a lie. He'd simply said I wasn't then fed me until I wanted to barf. And now more food was in the oven, tempting my nose as he picked out a movie.

While his back was turned, I felt my way to the couch, relieved that it was the only piece of furniture in the living room. It really was the perfect setup. For me. Some other woman would probably come in here and start asking for more chairs and other trip hazards.

"I think you'll like this one," Scath said, moving toward the dark shape on the wall. He bent down, and a moment later, the TV turned on.

It had been ages since I'd watched a movie. Longer still since I'd spent time with someone doing something non-essential. My dating life before the quakes had been pretty non-existent, and not because of my eyes. Back then, I'd had contacts.

I missed those contacts.

No, my dating woes had been due to being burned by man-whores too many times. I'd thought I'd found guys who wanted more than a quick fuck. The first one I'd caught sexting with three other women. The second one I'd found getting head in my living room from my neighbor.

Since then, I hadn't given men much time or consideration.

And I kind of missed the company, I realized as Scath sat next to me, his largeness consuming what remained of the couch space. His heat radiated against my side as the opening music played.

"Is this okay?" he asked. "I can look for more furniture if—"

"No," I said quickly. "This is perfect." As soon as I said it, I realized he might not like being so cozy and added, "Do you want me to sit on the floor so you're not crowded?"

"No," he said just as forcefully as I'd said it. He lifted his arm, setting it on the back of the couch to make some more room between us. "This is fine."

"Okay." I settled in and stared at the shifting colors on the TV. Thankfully, it was a movie with enough dialogue to figure out what was going on, and I was smiling a few minutes later as I visualized what was happening.

"You can't see, can you?" Scath asked.

Panic bolted through me. "W-what? Why would you say that? Of course, I can see."

He grunted, and I waited for him to say more, but he

didn't. Fear wrapped its cruel hand around my torso and squeezed. I struggled to breathe and tried to stay calm. Was he already trying to figure out how to get rid of me? The possibility made me feel sick.

"I know Fallor is looking for other women," I said in a rush. "But I swear I'll find a way to be useful to you. If you don't want sex, that's fine. I can be useful in other ways. I have tons of knowledge when it comes to women and will share anything. Just, please, please let me stay."

He sighed heavily but didn't respond.

"What are you thinking?" I asked.

"Many of my brothers are eager to find females of their own. Fallor is looking for women for them."

I wanted to believe him but couldn't quite trust it. We all knew why the fey wanted females. Sex and babies. But Scath made it clear he didn't want sex from me. So he had no reason to want to keep me then. Unless...

"Do you like men?" I asked.

The sound on the television stopped.

"Some of them," Scath said. "Garret and Ryan are nice. Dad and James are too."

"No, that's not what I meant. Are you sexually attracted to men?"

He made an odd noise beside me. "No."

I wasn't relieved. If he was gay, that meant he wouldn't kick me out for another woman. Straight meant he'd eventually see someone he liked, and that just wasn't going to work for me, especially now that he knew I couldn't see. I needed to bring Scath over to team Apryl.

"Okay, then what do you like about women?" I asked.

"Their minds and hearts and...bodies."

So everything. That didn't help me at all.

"If you could touch a female or talk to a female, which would you rather do?" I asked.

"Both?"

I rolled my eyes. "If you had to pick one, which would you pick?"

"Neither?"

The guy wasn't giving me anything to go off of. How was I supposed to seduce him if I didn't know what he liked?

I bit my bottom lip and wondered what he would do if I just climbed onto his lap and started grinding on him. The fey never got angry at a woman, but I'd never witnessed a woman coming onto a fey at the level I was considering.

"I did not mean to upset you by noticing you have weak eyes."

"You didn't. I'm fine. And I don't have weak eyes."

He grunted, and this time, I heard the doubt in it even though it sounded like every other grunt. Before I could reiterate that there wasn't a problem, he resumed the movie.

I sat there in nervous silence, trying to figure out what to do, until the timer on the oven beeped and startled me.

"Wait here," Scath said, pausing the show again.

He left me on the couch, and I listened to him pull the brownies out of the oven. Water splashed. Dishes clinked.

I realized he was cleaning up lunch and started to stand.

"Sit, Apryl."

I froze then slowly sank back down, not liking that he'd been watching me.

"I can help dry the dishes," I said as he continued to move around in the kitchen.

"I lived alone before coming here. Your company is enough compensation for the food and care you require. You don't need to do anything."

Guests didn't need to do anything. People who lived

together worked together to keep their home running. The fact that he wasn't letting me do anything was a clear message that this wasn't my home. It was his, and I was just his guest. How could I go from guest to more?

The water drained, and I saw his grey shape approaching a minute later.

"I have a piece of brownie on a plate for you. Would you like me to set it on your lap?"

Shame filled me. He obviously hadn't believed my denials. Mutely, I held out my hand. He pressed the plate into it and didn't let go until he knew I had it.

Wallowing in self-pity, I took my first bite even though I was still so full it hurt. The fudgy goodness soothed some of the frayed edges of my emotions, and as I slowly chewed my first bite, I decided nothing tasted better than warm brownies.

"Do you like it?" Scath asked.

"I love it. So much. Thank you for making it."

"You are welcome. If you want other sweets, I can make them for you if you will read the box for me again."

"These brownies should last me a while."

He started the show again. Rather than paying attention to it, I let my mind wander and considered my options. Scath knew I couldn't see but didn't seem overly bothered by it. When I'd realized it was a fey who'd offered me a place to stay, I'd thought he would reject me because I had a genetic flaw. But he hadn't been interested even before he realized I couldn't see. So, did that mean the fey wouldn't care about my shitty eyesight? As he'd pointed out, there were a lot of other fey looking for women. And if Scath didn't want me, now that I was here, I could try enticing one of the others before Scath found one he liked.

"What are the chances one of the other fey would be

interested in taking me in?" I asked just to double-check that I was understanding the situation.

"None."

Any hope that had formed deflated in a whoosh. Stuffing another bite of brownie into my mouth, I struggled not to tear up. It was fine. At least, now I knew where to put my efforts. Instead of looking for another fey, I needed to secure my place with the one beside me.

How?

Think.

A direct invitation hadn't worked. How could I tempt him when I didn't know what he liked? Find out what he liked, obviously. But how?

Scath knew I couldn't see, and he was being nice about it. Helpful even. Maybe I could use that in a way that would entice his interest in me as a female. Perhaps asking for his help finding something to wear as pajamas after I was already undressed? Or better yet, taking a shower and calling him to help me figure out which bottle was shampoo. What straight guy didn't like looking at boobs? Mine were still decent enough even if they were a little deflated from lack of food in recent months.

Since the fey didn't have a lot of experience with females, any boobs would probably be good boobs in their book. Hell, in the beginning, they'd walked around, asking women if they could see their babymakers.

That thought caught in my head.

How could I possibly flash that area in a believable way?

"Do you want another brownie?" Scath asked, bringing me back to reality.

I swallowed the last bite and shook my head.

"Thanks for offering, but I'm full. Would you mind giving

me a tour of the house? It'll be easier to move around once I know where everything is," I said, holding out my plate.

When he took that, I held out my hand and breathed a sigh of relief when his closed around mine.

Seduce Scath and ensure my place. I can do this, I thought, standing.

CHAPTER TEN

SCATH

I MARVELED AT THE FEEL OF APRYL'S SMALL, TREMBLING FINGERS against mine. How many times had I dreamed of having a female's willing touch? More than I could count.

Struggling to control the urge to pull her into my arms and hold her close, I helped her to her feet. Emily warned us that emotional attachments couldn't be rushed. She used Merdon and Hannah as an example. It had taken weeks for Hannah to forget her bad feelings and develop good feelings for Merdon.

Apryl would need time to see that she didn't need to offer her body in exchange for food and warmth. That this house was truly her home, no matter what. When she understood that, then her good feelings for me would come. I only needed to be patient and keep reassuring her that I wanted her here without sounding desperate. Yet, when my heart began to race at the thought of a day when Apryl would desire me, I didn't want to be patient. I wanted that now.

"It'll be helpful if you tell me what's in each room. Especially anything on the floor like rugs or low tables," she said, reminding me she'd wanted a tour of her new home.

Our home.

I looked around the space, noting once more how very few comforts there were. During one of Emily and Hannah's game nights, I'd bet the low table that had been in this room and lost it. The plants too.

"This room only has the couch, television, and the dresser full of movies beneath it. There are no rugs here. Or tables or plants. Should I find some?"

"Not for me. They're hard to see, and I tend to trip on them. Less is better in my fuzzy world."

My chest swelled with the knowledge I had made the perfect house for her. Accidentally, of course, but that didn't matter. She wouldn't find another fey house with as little as my house had.

She released my hand and slowly made her way around the couch then walked to the television. I watched her closely. She kept her head down to watch where she was walking. When she did look up, she slowed or stopped moving. What I'd mistaken for indifference I now saw as caution. She truly couldn't see well at all. I'd thought she'd been hiding her face from me when she'd read the directions on the box by holding it close to her nose.

Pride that I'd discovered the truth quickly dissolved into concern. If there was another breach, my Apryl wouldn't know where to run or which humans were good humans and which were infected. How had she survived the last breach?

I led her to the kitchen, and she used her hands to explore the length of the counter and the layout of the appliances. And once she understood where everything was, she opened the cupboards and felt inside them.

I stopped her from reaching into the knife drawer and made her promise never to try using them.

"If you're willing to cook for me, I'm willing to let you. But if I'm faced with a choice between starvation and cutting myself, I'm going to use a knife," she said with a hint of humor in her voice. "Don't worry. I'll be really careful."

She turned toward me and patted my chest. The contact ended too soon, though, when she turned toward the hallway.

"Is the bedroom that way?" she asked.

"Yes."

She held out her hand again. It didn't matter that she was only asking for help; it was still a request for my touch. I took her hand in mine and relished the contact as I led her down the hall, prolonging our connection by pausing at each door to explain the room and its contents or lack of them.

When we reached the master bedroom, she released my hand to explore the space on her own.

"Only the one bed in the house?" she asked, standing beside it.

"Yes."

"We're sharing then?"

"Yes?" I said uncertainly.

I could sleep on the floor near the bed, like Kerr did for Cassie at first, but hoped Apryl would allow me to hold her at night. Cassie said she felt safer when Kerr held her, and I wanted Apryl to feel safe here. I would only touch her curves a little...just enough to hold her...for her protection.

Apryl flashed a quick smile at me.

"You're willing to feed me and house me when no one else will. If you think I'm going to argue about sharing a bed with you, you're wrong. I'm grateful you're letting me stay."

I needed her to understand that having her here wasn't a hardship. No, it was the exact opposite—a gift. But would telling her so scare her away? I thought of Angel's warning and decided it probably would. What could I say then? Should I tell her I was grateful she was willing to stay? No, that made me sound unworthy of her. I settled for simple.

"I am glad you're staying."

She smiled again and reached for the bag she'd left in the room. I watched her unpack and frowned at how very little she had. My pulse started to beat faster as I realized the opportunity before me. Azio had provided Terri with clothes that he could see through. It had scared her, but my Apryl wouldn't know if the clothes she wore were see-through.

"Would you like me to get more clothes for you?" I asked.

"Oh, I don't want to trouble you."

"It's no trouble. I want you to feel comfortable here."

"If you're sure…"

"I am."

She shrugged and reached for the hem of her sweater.

"Do you mind if I do some laundry?" she asked.

"No."

She tugged the sweater off, and my mouth went dry when her shirt came with it. I stared at her warm skin and the grey bra pressing her breasts together so they touched in the middle. The connecting line taunted me as she unbuttoned her jeans and bent over to push them down her hips.

"I'll need you to show me how to use the washer and dryer," she said as the jeans joined the sweater and shirt.

Then she reached behind her. A second later, the material dam broke, and her breasts spilled free. The sight of her darker nipples held me captive until she reached for her underwear.

"I wasn't able to wash my clothes as often as I would have liked," she said.

I barely heard her. My ears rang with my own pulse as she lowered her last article of clothing. Completely bare, she stood in front of me. I struggled to breathe.

She was glorious. Curved and supple. Her breasts hung free, little lines marking their borders, highlighting their size.

My fingers itched to trace those stripes and hold the weight of those beautiful mounds.

My gaze had barely drifted lower to that thatch of dark hair between her legs when she turned and bent over to pick up her clothes. Her pretty pussy parted for my view, and I grunted at the forceful need that hit me. I wanted to fall to my knees and bury my tongue in those folds, lapping at her until she screamed my name and told me she loved me.

Swallowing hard, I turned away from the sight.

Patience, I reminded myself.

"I will wash your clothes for you," I said. "You can wear one of my shirts for now. It will cover more of you until your clothes are clean."

"Oh," she said, straightening. "Okay."

I hurried to the closet and took a moment to adjust my throbbing length. In all my dreams, I never imagined Apryl would simply undress in front of me. Was I a fool for covering all of that beauty up again when I'd just been thinking of clothes that would reveal more? Yes, I had to be a fool. A fool who would explode in his pants if she walked around our home in no clothes at all.

Half of me was tempted to tell her I had no shirts then place things on the floor for her to pick up just so I could see her pussy again. But that wasn't getting to know her mind. Only her body. And if I wanted to know her mind, I needed to cover her body, or I wouldn't be able to focus.

Collecting a shirt, I left the closet and saw she'd placed the dirty clothes on the bed. With her hands held in front of her, she looked nervous. Did she regret taking off her clothes? I hoped not. It had been the second-best moment of my life. The best was still when she'd agreed to live with me.

I held out the shirt and tried not to look at her tempting

body. Instead of taking it, she raised her arms over her head. The move lifted her breasts high.

I stared again. I couldn't help myself. The need to touch her, to caress those dark peaks until they tightened in need, clawed at me.

"Can you help me?" she asked.

I couldn't speak. Could barely move. So I grunted and looked down at the shirt in an attempt to collect my thoughts.

With numb fingers, I threaded her hands through the arm openings and eased the material over her head. Unable to stop, I skimmed my fingers over her breasts as I pulled the shirt down to cover her mouthwatering pussy.

"Thanks," she breathed, smoothing a small hand over each breast.

I wanted to beg to do that for her. Instead, I turned away and picked up her clothes.

"I will wash these," I rasped.

"Wait. Show me how."

I grunted, and she followed me. The controls on the washer were clearly marked and easy for her to adjust by feel. After seeing where I kept the soap and dryer sheets, she assured me she wouldn't need me to help her with laundry again.

"I don't mind helping you, Apryl," I said so she would know she wasn't a burden.

She made a small humming sound, then asked, "Should we finish watching the movie?"

"How do you watch it if you cannot see it?"

"I listen. There might even be an option for audio description, which means a voice will tell me what's happening on the screen."

"I will tell you what's happening," I said, embracing any reason to talk to her.

We sat together on the couch and started the movie again. I

told her what was happening, and she moved close to me, pressing against my side and resting a hand on my chest. It distracted me a little, and I missed describing a few things. My focus dissolved further when her hand drifted to my stomach, but I still managed to speak without interruption until her hand landed on my cock.

Aching and seconds from thrusting into her palm, I bolted from my seat and accidentally knocked her over. Her legs spread wide, giving me another enticing view of her sweet pussy.

"We need more eggs to eat pussy. Waffles! To eat waffles. I will go find some."

I ran.

CHAPTER ELEVEN

APRYL

I LISTENED TO THE DOOR SLAM AND RUBBED A HAND DOWN MY face as I straightened from my sprawled position on the couch. My attempts at seduction had played out like a slapstick comedy rather than anything sexy, and I didn't blame Scath for bolting. Since when did falling over involve air splits? Never, that's when. Yet, I'd done it.

Lifting my head, I peered down at my thatch. I should have thought things through and shaved first. Maybe my current Amazonian state was what had sent him running. He'd seemed calm enough when I'd stripped in front of him under the pretext of wanting to do laundry, but the moment I'd bent over to pick it up, he'd hustled away to get me a shirt.

What was it he'd said again?

Oh yeah, "You can wear one of my shirts for now. It will cover more of you until your clothes are clean."

For a guy who claimed to be straight, he sure was acting like he had zero interest in the female body. Or maybe just my body.

Unable to afford that kind of negativity, I shook the thought from my head and tried to regroup. Obviously, flashing Scath hadn't worked any better than a blatant invitation for sex. Since the brazen approach wasn't working, I needed to try something more discreet. Maybe he needed to be mentally seduced instead of physically. I had to think of the long game.

The thought barely settled into my mind when I realized my problem. The fey didn't do casual. Ever. They wanted the long game. Wifey, kids, white-picket fence...the whole package. The implications of that end result hit me. If I succeeded in getting him into bed, was I ready to be his female in every way that entailed?

I exhaled heavily, not seeing any other choice. He said there weren't any other fey who wanted me. I just wished I understood why, especially when he didn't seem to want me. I knew it had nothing to do with skin color. Some of the fey were darker than me. And it had nothing to do with my eyesight. He'd invited me to live with him before he figured out I couldn't see well. And I doubted it had anything to do with my personality. He didn't even know me. When I'd met him this morning, I had been—

My mouth dropped open into a little 'O'.

I'd been trying to kiss Fallor.

I wanted to smack myself. Of course, he wasn't interested in me when I'd tried kissing another one of them right in front of him only a few hours ago.

Yep, seduction would have to wait a few days. But it wouldn't hurt to prepare for that phase while I brainstormed how to win Scath over. I definitely needed to switch tactics—again—to convince Scath that I wasn't into Fallor.

Heaving a sigh, I got up and started navigating the house on my own. The three-bedroom ranch was sparsely furnished, which I liked. And he only seemed to use one of the two bathrooms, which could lead to some cozy intimacy like brushing our teeth together in the evenings. Plus, this place had an outdoor woodstove, which kept the house at a temperature that allowed me to comfortably walk around without underwear.

Walking around pantsless was a novelty I enjoyed.

As was the electric shaver I found under the sink in the master bathroom. I held the device in my hand and debated the wisdom of what I was about to try. I couldn't see what I was doing. Even if I had my glasses, I had too much tit in the way, and shaving blind was a very dangerous thing. Yet, Scath had already run at the sight of my cooch critter twice. If he ever caught a glimpse of it again, I couldn't give him a third reason to run. It needed to go.

Praying I wouldn't nick something and need triage, I hiked a foot onto the counter and got to work. Fifteen minutes later, I ran my hand over my ravaged—not in a good way—fun zone. The short and bumpy, narrow strip I'd created felt like an Alaskan runway. No doubt, it looked like I'd used a weedwhacker to create it, and the sight of it would probably send Scath scurrying faster than the last time…if he saw it like this.

The hack job just provided me with more incentive to keep it covered and try the really, really subtle approach. I glanced down at what looked like a puppy's worth of fur-blur on the floor and cringed. He was going to know exactly what I'd been doing if I couldn't figure out how to clean that up.

I found a broom in the kitchen closet and spent another few minutes sweeping and praying that I got it all. From the floor. I could feel that I still had plenty of stubble between my legs every time I bent over.

The front door opened long after I put on my spare pair of underwear, changed over the laundry, and put away the brownies.

From my seat at the table, I couldn't discern if the grey and tan shape was Scath's or another fey's.

"Scath? Is that you?" I asked nervously.

"Yes. I have more food."

"You didn't need to do that. I'm sorry I made you so uncomfortable that you needed to leave. I promise that won't happen again. I put on some underwear."

He grunted and moved toward the kitchen.

"Did you still want to finish watching that movie with me?" I asked.

"Yes."

Relieved he wasn't going to try to avoid me, I hurried to the living room, more confident with my surroundings, and sat on my half of the couch. He joined me, but not on the couch. He brought in a chair from the table and placed it a healthy distance away from me.

His avoidance made me feel even worse about what I'd done.

"Did anyone ever mention a movie theater to you?" I asked, hoping he'd see conversation as the olive branch it was.

"No. What is a movie theater?"

"It's a large building that has screens, like the tv but way bigger, that would show new movies. It allowed a lot of people to watch the movie at the same time. And there would be concessions like popcorn and candy. There's something about watching a movie with a crowd, the collective reactions, that made it a really cool experience."

"Do you miss that?"

"The idea of going to the movies? Not really. I wouldn't enjoy them as much now without my glasses or contacts. And I definitely have an aversion to crowds after the last few months. But I do miss people. That probably doesn't make sense, but having friends…people to talk to when I'm feeling down or worrying about something? I do miss that. A lot."

"You can talk to me."

I offered him a small smile.

"All right. Is now a good time? Because I'm really feeling down about something that happened recently and could use someone to talk to."

"Yes, tell me."

"Well, I think I made a fool of myself. There's this really nice guy who offered me a place to stay—"

Scath growled. When I frowned, the sound cut off.

"You okay?" I asked, unsure that I'd really heard what I thought I'd heard.

"You are staying with me, Apryl," he said forcefully.

"Uh, yeah. That's not the point of this story."

"Okay. Continue."

Not sure what to think of his weird behavior, I cleared my throat and tried again. "After he opened his home to me and made me feel very welcome, I think I got a little too comfortable. I'm sorry I walked around your house without underwear on, Scath. I didn't mean to make you so uncomfortable that you had to leave. I didn't mean to make you uncomfortable at all."

Silence answered me, and that awkward feeling grew inside of me. The need to speak, to say something else to try to smooth things over, nearly strangled me, but I managed to keep my mouth shut and wait for his reaction.

"So no other man asked you to live with him?" he said finally.

"No, the story was about you."

"Ah."

"That's it? Ah."

He brushed his hand over the back of mine. The

unexpected touch at such a tense moment made me jump a little, and he exhaled heavily.

"I do not wear underwear, Apryl. They pinch and bind and are uncomfortable. You should not wear them if you do not want to."

"Oh." I wanted to ask him why he bolted then but stopped myself as another possibility slid into place. The way he'd said "pussy" instead of waffles hadn't escaped my notice. I'd just figured he'd said the word because of what I'd been flashing him. What if he'd been saying it for another reason? The way he'd growled when he'd mistakenly thought I was talking about another guy sure suggested it.

Did that mean that Scath was interested then? Were my overt attempts to seduce him just too much? Testing my theory that subtlety was the key, I held out my hand.

His immediately closed over mine, threading our fingers together.

"I want to believe that I didn't upset you, but you just about ran out of the house, and now you won't sit by me. It makes me feel like I did something you didn't like."

"No. I like everything you do, Apryl."

"Then why won't you sit by me?"

Still holding my hand, he stood and claimed the space next to me. I brought his hand to my chest to hug it.

"So you were okay with everything?" I asked.

"Yes."

Was it just me, or had his answer sounded clipped? Was I making him uncomfortable again?

"Thank you for understanding," I said. "If I do anything that makes you uncomfortable, will you tell me? I want to be a good roommate."

"You are good, Apryl. Very good."

I smiled and brought his hand to my mouth, placing a soft kiss on his knuckles.

"I will start the movie," Scath said, easing himself from my hold.

When he returned with the remote, I snuggled up against him.

"Is this okay?" I asked.

"Yes."

He sounded unsure but didn't bolt.

Go slow, I reminded myself.

So I threaded my fingers through his and just held his hand for a bit as I listened to the movie. It was kind of nice being this cozy with another person.

After a while, I lifted his arm and ducked under it so I could lean directly against his side with his arm over my shoulders. He didn't protest or try to pull away. So I made myself comfortable.

The ridge of his defined pectoral against my cheek distracted me from the conversation on the television and brought my attention to exactly how muscled he was. Too curious to deny myself, I released his hand and lightly set mine against his side. He twitched under me but didn't say anything.

"Am I making myself too comfortable?" I asked, needing to know if I was pushing too far again.

"No. This is…fine."

He'd hesitated. Why had he hesitated? Just how slow did I need to go with this guy? The clock was ticking to secure my place here, and my fingers were itching to explore that expanse of chest beneath my cheek.

Exhaling slowly, I readjusted my seduction game plan and tried not to think of the grooming effort I'd probably wasted.

CHAPTER TWELVE

SCATH

EACH OF HER EXHALES WARMED MY CHEST AND TEASED MY NIPPLE. My cock throbbed in time with my pulse. A smarter male would have stayed in the chair, but when she'd looked at me with her big, sad eyes and held out her hand, I couldn't refuse to comfort her. And because of that, I would be comforting my aching balls later.

She moved against me, rubbing her breast against my side, and I released my hold on the remote when I heard a faint click in my hand. I tried not to remember what her pussy had looked like when she'd fallen over. How it had glistened with moisture... How it would probably feel squeezing around my cock...

The hand she had resting on my side moved, inching slowly over my ribs, scalding a path and igniting a level of need that would see me spilling in my pants.

"I'm thirsty. Are you thirsty?" I asked quickly, detangling myself from her.

"Sure. I guess," she said, sounding confused.

She hadn't liked when I'd left the house before, and I knew she felt the same about me leaving the couch, but I didn't know what else to do. I wanted her touches and smiles and sweet looks; however, I only wanted them if she wanted to give them, not because she felt she had to. And although her apology had seemed sincere, no women were ever that comfortable showing their pussy to one of us. It wasn't natural. I wanted it to be. Desperately. And that was why I couldn't take what she was offering.

Not one look.

Not one touch.

Not one lick.

A soft groan rumbled through my chest as I removed two glasses from the cupboards. I would give anything to bury my face between her legs and lick her slit until she begged me to stop. My hands shook as I filled the first glass then the second.

"Do you want a snack?" I asked.

"No. I'm still full from lunch. I'm not used to eating that much."

I pictured her on her knees, looking up at my cock, licking her lips, then saying that. Swallowing my frustrated growl, I strode to the living room and closed her hand around the glass.

"I'll be right back," I said. Before I made it more than a few steps, I paused and added, "I need to use the bathroom," so she would know I wasn't running away again.

In the master bathroom, I grabbed the conditioner from the shower and squeezed a healthy amount into my palm while I pulled my cock free. Slicking the cool liquid over my length, I thrust into my fist. The image of Apryl bent over in front of me, the white edge of the t-shirt brushing the top of her ass cleft and leaving her fully exposed to me, did me in.

I came with a grunt, embracing the tingling itch in my balls as stream after stream jetted into my palm and fell with loud splats into the toilet. When it finally finished, I exhaled slowly, noting my chest didn't feel as tight as it had a moment ago. And my hands didn't shake as I washed them.

Feeling more controlled and relaxed, I left the bathroom and returned to the living room. Apryl was no longer sitting on the couch but stood near the sink in the kitchen. Her empty glass sat on the counter next to mine.

"You didn't need to return it. I would have done that for you," I said.

"I'm not helpless, Scath. I might not be able to cook over an open flame without starting something on fire, but I can bring my cup to the sink."

"I know you are not helpless," I said, unsure why she was upset. Did she think I was going to ask her to cook dinner when she had already told me that she wasn't good at it?

"There are sweet treats in the freezer you can eat without cooking if you're hungry," I said.

"I'm not. Thank you for offering, though."

She sounded less upset now, which relieved me. I didn't know her mind well enough to guess how to soothe her when I didn't even understand the problem.

"Would you like to keep watching the movie?" I asked.

"Sure." She moved to the couch, and I followed. However, when she reached it, she motioned for me to sit first.

"I appreciate you telling me what was going on. For a second there, I thought you were running again," she said as she tucked herself against my side.

Was that why she was upset? Because I'd left her even for a moment? Pleased with the thought she was already growing attached, I slipped my arm over her shoulders like before.

Only this time, my palm skimmed over her breast.

I jerked my hand back.

"Forgive me, Apryl. I didn't mean to touch you without your permission."

"You have my permission, Scath. Already told you that. There's no need to freak out. Here." She grabbed my hand and placed it over her breast again, using her fingers to close mine over that enticingly soft mound.

My cock stirred.

"See? I'm not freaking out, and you're not freaking out. We're fine. Right?" she said, looking up at me with those big, warm eyes.

I grunted instead of wheezing in need, and she smiled.

"I'll take that as a 'yes, we're fine.' Seriously, I don't mind touching. It's something I've kind of missed. To keep everyone from guessing that I couldn't see, I pretended to be shy and let people think I preferred being alone. I don't. I missed the contact. A lot."

Was that why she kissed Fallor? She was hungry for contact and not because she was using her body to trade for food? What she had said to Fallor rang in my head.

"Anything you want. Kissing. A blow job. Sex. It's yours."

June explained the contact females wanted first. Hand holding and hugs. Kissing, blow jobs, and sex came when females loved a male. I knew Apryl didn't love me. Not yet. So she was still offering her body out of fear.

"We are fine," I said, easing my hand away from her breast. "You can hug my side as long as you want."

I turned the movie on again, no longer remembering the story it was trying to tell. My thoughts were too twisted around Apryl's story and how to help her understand that I didn't want her body until I had her heart.

She sighed and settled against my side, her breathing once more teasing my skin. The previous need I felt slowly crawled down my spine, teasing my balls and stirring my cock as the movie progressed. I did my best to ignore it, but then her fingers started exploring the material of my shirt, rubbing back and forth over it, creeping steadily across my chest, feeding that ache.

I almost removed her hand but thought better of it. Perhaps allowing her to touch me would encourage her mind and heart to welcome me as well. So I sat still when her fingers brushed over my nipple and down my chest. My breathing sped when she reached my stomach and smoothed her hand over the muscles there. But when she started going lower, I couldn't take any more.

Gently lifting her hand, I slipped out from under her and stood.

"I must use the bathroom again," I said, hurrying away.

The conditioner was still on the counter. I ripped my pants down, wet my palm, and frantically stroked my cock. Only this time, I imagined I hadn't stopped her exploration and it was her hand slipping up and down my shaft. Her mouth closing over the head. Her throat working as she swallowed—

I hissed out a breath as my balls tightened and the first spurt of my seed hit my palm. Twitching, I rode out my release then caught my breath before washing my hands. If I continued to use the conditioner this frequently, I would be out by morning. Sooner if Apryl fell down and showed her pussy again. I could check the supply shed for another bottle but didn't want to leave when it seemed to upset her.

Did I still have a bottle of lotion under the sink?

Bending down to check, I noticed a dusting of hair clippings on the floor. Dark hair, like mine, but with a slight curl to the short pieces. Frowning, I tried to recall Apryl's hair. Had she cut it? Why only little bits, though?

I opened the door and saw the clippers there. Mom explained they were for men like Dad, who had facial hair. Angel said they were handy to keep for women who might not have shaved their legs for a while. I didn't care if a woman's legs were fuzzy or bare, but if Apryl wanted to remove the hair from them, then I was happy I'd kept the shaver.

Inspecting the contents of the cabinet and finding no lotion, I stood and considered my options. Not allowing Apryl to touch me wasn't one of them. And how I responded was impossible to ignore; I'd release in my pants if I tried. Relieving the pressure was the only way. The conditioner was almost gone, and she would notice if I took several showers in a short period of time. Stroking myself wouldn't be as pleasant without the conditioner, but for her, I'd manage.

Resolute, I left the bathroom and returned to the living room. She was in the kitchen again, this time bent over in front of the freezer. To my disappointment, I saw she truly had put on underwear.

"Are you hungry?" I asked.

"Maybe," she said, straightening with one of the colorful sweet sticks. She peeled the wrapper away and smiled at me. "I haven't had something like this in my mouth in ages."

She parted her lips and slid the treat into her mouth. The red-colored tip disappeared and she moaned around the end before pulling it out with a wet pop.

"So good," she said a second before she sucked it in again, this time taking more. Half the white portion disappeared between her lips. Her tongue darted out, licking along the bottom almost to the blue section at the end.

She withdrew it only to insert it again. And again. Sucking. Slurping. Going deeper each time.

The throb in my cock returned, and I gripped the counter as my hips bucked. I couldn't make myself leave. I couldn't even look away.

She opened wider, and the whole treat disappeared between her lips for a moment before she pulled it free of her lips completely.

"This is so juicy. I didn't know how much I'd love sucking on it. Are there any other big, delicious things for me to suck around here?"

My balls began to tingle as I imagined just what I could offer her.

"I'll be right back," I said in a rush before I hurried to the bathroom.

CHAPTER THIRTEEN

APRYL

I COULDN'T BELIEVE I WAS LYING IN BED—THE ONLY BED IN THE house—alone. I'd been so sure I'd grabbed his attention in a sexual way after showing him how I could deepthroat a popsicle. But then he'd bolted, and after that, he'd had one excuse after another not to sit with me to finish the movie.

Dinner needed to be made since I was hungry.

The laundry had to be switched over.

I needed more clothes, so he ran to the supply shed—I'd gotten an awkward side hug before he left, though, and a stern warning that I couldn't live with anyone else.

When he'd returned, he acted like he was super tired. I'd jumped on that like a starving woman on a chocolate sundae. But once he'd tucked me in, literally, he'd left the room, saying he would sleep on the couch.

Scath was running so hot and cold that I didn't know up from down. Was he into me, or was I just getting all my signals mixed? It was just too hard to tell.

Sighing, I rolled over in bed and tried to fall asleep. It wasn't working, though. I couldn't stop worrying about what would happen when more girls started showing up here courtesy of Fallor. I was lucky one hadn't already.

Throwing back the covers, I got out of bed and made my way to the living room. Everything was dark, and I moved around with a hand on the wall so I'd know where I was. When I reached the living room, I heard Scath shift on the couch.

"Are you hungry?" he asked.

"No. I can't sleep. I'm not used to a quiet house like this. Can you sleep next to me? Please?"

I heard a rustle of noise and stayed right where I was.

"Yes. I will sleep next to you," he said from nearby.

"Thank you." I turned, switched hands on the wall, and started toward the bedroom.

"Can you see anything?" he asked behind me.

"No. Not when it's this dark."

A second later, I was up in his arms.

"You don't have to carry me. As long as you're not adding or rearranging furniture, I can get around fine."

He grunted and continued walking. In his arms wasn't the worst place to be. His biceps pressed against my back and thighs while my shoulder rubbed his hard chest. He was all muscly and touchable, but I didn't try to explore with my fingers again. I didn't want him to avoid me more.

Pausing, he leaned forward and lowered me to the bed. Before I could reach for the quilt, he pulled it up to cover me. Maybe it was my imagination, but I could have sworn I felt his fingers brush over my cheek before I heard him walk around the bed.

The mattress dipped. Rolling to my side, I faced him. I couldn't see him, but based on how the mattress had moved, I knew he was at the other edge.

"Can I ask you a question?" I asked softly.

"Yes."

"You didn't know I couldn't see until after you already made it clear you didn't want sex. So why don't you want me?"

I tried to keep the hurt and fear from my voice but didn't fully succeed. It didn't feel good knowing I was completely unwanted by everyone.

Scath was quiet for a long moment then exhaled heavily and rolled toward me.

"You offer touches and sex as payment for food and shelter, Apryl. Refusing them isn't rejection; it's compassion. You are not a burden. You owe me nothing for living here. Now, sleep."

I bit my lip and considered his words. Humans weren't nice. The majority of men would take me up on what I offered. But Scath wasn't human. The fey didn't play around. They wanted forever…with the right woman. While Scath clarified that he wasn't rejecting me, what he'd said certainly wasn't a declaration of any kind of feelings for me either.

"I'm afraid another woman will come along and I'll end up in the snow," I said honestly.

"That won't happen."

"You already said no other fey will take me in, and I can promise you that no humans want my level of inept either." I swallowed hard, trying not to let my emotions get the better of me.

"Go to sleep, Apryl. You're tired."

He wasn't wrong. I knew my exhaustion was contributing to some of the misery I felt as I rolled away from him and closed my eyes. But knowing it didn't stop my tears from quietly rolling down my cheeks.

I sniffled.

An arm snaked around my waist, and Scath slowly drew

me across the bed until my back pressed against his hard, chiseled chest.

"I want you to stay here with me, Apryl. But I won't force you. If you wish to live with another one of my brothers, any of them will take you in."

I twisted to look back at him.

"But you said…"

"I want you to stay here," he repeated.

I realized what he was saying. He'd lied to me. I wasn't rejected. I'd never been so relieved to have been lied to in my life. He'd said none of the other fey would take me in because he wanted me. A weight lifted off of me, and my tears slowed just before confusion settled in. If he wanted me, why did he keep turning me away? Was he really that noble that he'd rather have nothing at all than accept what I offered as payment to stay here? Why did it matter to him so much? He could have saved me a day of anguish.

The selfish level of my thoughts hit me hard. Yes, he could have saved me anguish, but what about him? Fey didn't do casual hookups. Doing anything with me would have felt like a lie to him, especially when he knew why I was doing it.

He wanted the real deal from me. Romance. Love.

Could I give that to him? A real relationship?

Thinking it just felt weird. Not due to what he was or how he looked, though. None of that really bothered me since I couldn't see it. The problem was my frame of mind. It was still hardwired in survival mode. It seemed silly to emotionally invest in someone when the population could be cut in half on any given day.

But not here. Not with him. He'd keep me safe.

The fey always kept their females safe.

I exhaled heavily and placed my hand over his.

"Thank you." I wasn't even sure what I was thanking him

for. I only knew that I was grateful. Grateful for the relief I now felt. For the roof over my head. For the food he was willing to share and for his kind consideration.

"Sleep," he said softly.

Sighing, I finally gave in to the need.

When I woke in the morning, I was alone in bed. Sunlight poured into the space from the opened curtains, and I blinked at the whiteness above me as I reflected on the prior day. So much had happened in just a short period of time that I hadn't really considered what living with a fey would mean. I didn't need to rush out of the house. I didn't need to stand in a food line and find ways not to be noticed. But that also meant that I didn't have a clue what I was supposed to do.

Based on the conversations I'd overheard while living in Tenacity, everyone held the same belief that hooking up with a fey meant non-stop sex. That's why so many women hadn't jumped on the dinner date option. The food was tempting, but spending the rest of their days on their backs was not.

Considering the way Scath had turned me down, the rumor about their sex drive was obviously inflated. I frowned as doubt returned. What if it wasn't? What if he just wasn't that into me?

Shaking my head, I told myself to calm down and got out of bed.

I took my time to straighten the blankets and then used the bathroom and found a new toothbrush in a wrapper waiting on the counter, along with a brand-new tube of toothpaste. Smiling, I used both before searching out Scath.

All I needed to do was follow my nose. The scent of bacon set my stomach rumbling.

"That smells amazing," I said, entering the kitchen.

"Bacon is one of my favorite meats. June says that bacon and Spam come from the same animal."

"Yep. Pigs. I try not to think about the animal, though. Makes eating it less enjoyable."

"Why?"

"Because I feel sad that it died and I'm eating it, I guess."

"Emily feels the same way. She said she used to only eat vegetables."

I grinned at the disbelief in his voice.

"A lot of people choose to eat only vegetables and live healthy and happy lives. Not all vegetables taste like peas, you know. And considering the lack of animals around here, you might need to get used to eating more greens."

The stove clicked off.

"Come with me," he said, taking my hand.

I let him lead me through the house to the garage. The cement was freezing on my bare feet, but I didn't complain when something creaked and he set my hand on cold paper lumps. I ran my fingers over package after package of wrapped meat then felt the outside of the freezer to gauge how big it was as he closed the top. It was enough to feed both of us for at least two years.

"Does everyone here have this much meat?" I asked

"Yes."

"Where does it come from? I heard that there isn't a lot of meat found when the humans go out for supply runs."

He led me back into the house as he answered.

"Not many humans go on supply runs. Those who do only find a portion of what's there. When we go out on our own, we don't leave as quickly and remove everything we can from the home."

"I imagine I'd linger and find more if I weren't terrified of being bitten, too."

His arms wrapped around me, stopping me in my tracks.

"You do not need to go on supply runs, Apryl. Tell me what you need, and I will get it for you."

I let myself lean into his embrace and shook my head.

"I don't need anything right now. I'm just thinking about all the poor people who were brave enough to go on supply runs in the first place. I can't imagine the amount of courage it took them to step up like that. And to know that their efforts weren't good enough. That you could find way more on your own. That's a little bit of a punch to the middle."

"I don't understand."

"The fey are superior in every way. You're faster, strong, and immune. Of course, you'll find more supplies when we're weaker, slower, and terrified out of our minds. But the ones who were going out? They were still trying. And not just for themselves but for everyone back at their assigned houses who weren't brave enough to go out, like me. It just makes me feel really bad for them and really guilty that I'm here now, eating like a queen when I did absolutely nothing to earn it."

I tipped my head back and looked up at his blurry face.

"I hate being useless."

"You are not useless, Apryl, and I will prove it to you."

CHAPTER FOURTEEN

SCATH

I HATED THE SADNESS REFLECTED IN HER EXPRESSION. IT REMINDED me of her tears the previous night before I pulled her into my arms. Sleeping beside Apryl had been everything I'd hoped it would be. She had fit perfectly against me, the softness of her backside molding against my hips like a lock to my key.

We were meant to be together. I knew it in my heart. But not only because of how she felt in my arms.

She was resilient, enduring when a more fragile person would have given up. And more courageous than she understood. She willingly came to live with a fey when so many refused out of fear. In Apryl, I saw a female who was made to survive this world. Made for me.

Not Fallor or any other fey. Just me.

If only she would see that.

I dipped my head to inhale her scent then led her to the kitchen. She sat when I pulled out the stool for her and rested her chin in her hand as I went to the stove.

"See?" she said. "I wouldn't even be able to make my own plate right now without burning myself on hot grease. Back in Tenacity, I didn't have to worry about it. Everyone was so uptight about splitting the food equally that I never had to make my own plate. I only had to accept whatever was handed to me."

I looked down at the plate of food I was about to give her and changed my mind. If I wanted Apryl to see herself as I did, I would need to stop doing everything for her. My insides twisted at the thought. I yearned to care for her in every way possible. To show her I was the perfect male for her. But her independence and feelings of self-worth were more important than my need to give her everything.

Instead of serving her, I plated the bacon and eggs separately and set them in front of her before handing her an empty plate.

"You can serve yourself. The bacon isn't too hot."

She blinked at me and shifted her gaze to the plates.

"Is there something to scoop up the eggs?" she asked.

I took a bright red plastic spoon from the container by the stove and set it on the plate. Her smile stole my breath.

"I love that," she said, picking up the spoon. "Bright, contrasting colors make it easier to distinguish what I'm looking at."

She served herself some eggs and took a small portion of bacon before looking up at me.

"You're eating too, right?" she asked.

I fixed a plate for myself and joined her, my arm brushing hers as we ate. When we finished, I reached for her plate.

"I can clean up since you cooked," she said.

"All right. But not the pans. I'll do those."

She smiled again, and I talked her through where to find the dish soap and washcloths.

"Would you like a tour of Tolerance today?" I asked as I watched her.

"Actually, I'd love that. A lot."

After she'd stacked the clean, dry plates on the counter, she went to change. While she did that, I finished cleaning up.

"Hey, Scath? Where did you put the clothes you brought home yesterday?" Apryl called from the bedroom.

I froze, thinking of the clothes I'd put in the closet. My mind had been on Apryl's beautiful breasts and pussy when I'd run to the supply shed. The thin shirts and very small shorts weren't anything I wanted her to wear on the tour.

I hurried down the hallway and entered the bedroom just as she left the closet.

She already had one of the shirts on. And the orange underwear I'd picked out.

"You have great taste," she said. "As a thong girl before the earthquakes, you can imagine my disappointment over what I'd been wearing. These are perfect. And the shirt is so soft." She ran her hands down her sides. "Did you see my bra? Going without around the house is fine with me, but I'd rather have something on when we go out."

Torn with indecision, I stared at her dark nipples through the transparent shirt. I didn't want her to cover up, but I didn't want anyone else to see her either. My gaze drifted down her waist to the bright orange triangle. Her pretty patch of hair no longer tufted out around the material like the last time.

My gaze flew to her head and I frowned with the sudden understand that she hadn't cut the hair there. She'd cut it down *there*. But how much remained now? I had liked those curls very much.

"Scath?"

"Yes?" I answered roughly.

"Do you see my bra anywhere?"

"No," I said. And I hoped never to see it again. "You will be fine without it. The jacket will cover you and keep you warm."

She chuckled and went back into the closet.

"I know the jacket will keep me warm. The bra is all about support so the girls aren't flopping around."

The idea of them moving vigorously made me hard, and I palmed myself. We needed more conditioner. Or lotion. Anything.

Then she bent at the waist to step into her jeans, reminding me why, at some point in the night, I'd run out of conditioner. The smooth curve of her exposed ass and the memory of that sweet backside pressed up against my cock did me in.

"I'll be right back. I have to go to the bathroom."

I closed the door between us and roughly stroked myself until I released Panting, I stood there for a moment before washing my hands and straightening my pants.

When I left the bathroom, she was no longer in the bedroom but putting on her jacket by the door. Covered from head to toe, she was just as adorable but easier to look at without my pants trying to strangle my cock.

"Ready?" she asked.

Nodding, I led her outside.

The tour took time. She asked questions about the house and the streets and often paused to ask where we were in comparison to my house. After correcting her for the third time that it was "our" home, not mine, she started saying it correctly.

She held my hand as we walked, and her possession of it made me feel complete. Needed. It didn't matter that she only needed me because she couldn't see. She still needed me.

While I was focused on Apryl at my side, I was also aware of my brothers. They nodded to me as we passed, even as they spoke of Ryan's efforts to find another subdivision for a new community. I understood the yearning and joy in their expressions as they watched Apryl walk beside me. I'd felt the same every time I watched Shax carry Angel, big and round with the baby, through the settlement. Seeing another one of us with a female was hope that more would join us. And another settlement meant more opportunities to pair with females looking for a new home.

"Am I hearing cows?" Apryl asked when we neared the grassy area we used as a pasture.

"Yes."

"Are these the ones from Tenacity, or did you find more?"

"These are the same ones." The herd had been split between Tenacity and Tolerance initially. However, a cow had disappeared from Tenacity within a few days. Matt told Mya that he believed the people had butchered it secretly. Rather than risk more, he'd asked Mya to take the remaining cattle.

"I can't believe they're still alive," Apryl said. "After Matt announced they would be moved for everyone's safety, there were a lot of rumors that the cows hadn't actually been taken by infected."

"The infected would take people, not cows," I said. "Matt knew that, too, and only supported the rumor that it was an infected so those who ate the animal wouldn't be able to argue about sending the cattle away."

"Huh. That's pretty smart of him. I'm betting it was the group that just got kicked out. If they were willing to beat people and steal their food, they wouldn't have a problem killing a cow. How did no one else notice, though?"

"Many people were afraid of Nat and his men."

"True. That's why I missed out on the first food line. I heard the angry shouting and went back home."

"You will never go without food again," I promised.

She smiled up at me. "Not with cows roaming around. Can we go see them?"

After she listened to the cows for a while and patted one's

side, we continued the tour. She didn't want to stop at anyone's house to say hello—she wasn't ready yet—but did want to explore the supply shed.

I took one of the plastic bags Mom had near the door and added a new bottle of conditioner and lotion to it while Apryl looked through the spare clothes.

"I can't tell what I'm looking at," she said with a hint of frustration in her voice. "I want something that will look nice for when I'm ready to meet the other women you mentioned."

Moving to her side, I helped her pick out a sweater that was soft and pretty.

"Thank you, Scath," she said, hugging my arm as I tucked the sweater into the bag.

"Do you want anything else?"

"Maybe some more thongs if they have extras."

I eagerly found the shelf of them and took three more that I thought would fit her.

"What do you think?" she asked, touching them. "Or should I wear something more conservative?" She picked up a large white pair that would completely hide her ass and pussy.

My gaze drifted back to the thongs with longing. The bright triangles were made to grace her beautiful curves.

"You should wear whatever makes you the most comfortable," I said.

She frowned slightly and dropped the thongs into the bag.

"I love wearing thongs. They make me feel pretty and are comfortable at the same time."

Relief swept through me that she'd chosen the thongs, and when she held out her hand, I immediately wrapped my fingers around hers.

"Are you ready to head back and make me lunch?" she asked.

"Yes."

CHAPTER FIFTEEN

APRYL

WHEN HE'D SAID HE WOULD PROVE I WASN'T USELESS, I HADN'T expected him to go out of his way to help me feel useful. Showing me around town and teaching me how to navigate my new home was only the tip of the mountain of kindness he'd extended. He'd also found ways to help include me in our lunch preparation. Small things like showing me where the plates and silverware were kept so I could set our places and tasting the dish to tell him if it needed more salt. And his patience was endless when I couldn't find something or had trouble. Instead of doing it for me, he'd coach me through it.

Being involved, even on that small level, made me feel better. But that niggling worry about his interest in me remained in the back of my mind.

During the tour, he'd held my hand willingly enough after I'd initiated it but hadn't tried to pull me closer or anything like that. And when we'd reached the storage shed and I'd asked if I should pick out more thongs or plain, non-sexy underwear, he hadn't voiced any preference. If the guy was into me, he'd have a preference, wouldn't he?

The fey were always asking to see pussy. I'd heard a few

pose the question myself, so I knew it was really a thing. Scath hadn't asked to see mine yet. Granted, I'd flashed it at him twice on the first day together without prompting. Maybe that was the problem. Maybe he hadn't liked it. It had been a bit of a jungle down there. Maybe that had scared him away.

Unsure what to think, I paused behind him while he was transferring the noodle dish to a bowl at the counter so I could serve myself. After hesitating for only a moment, I wrapped my arms around him from behind and hugged my breasts to his back.

"Thank you for this. Including me really does make me feel like less of a waste of space."

"You do not waste space," he said firmly, his hand patting my arm. "For dinner, you will help me make your grandma's fighting meatballs."

His promise took away from the sting of disappointment over the arm pat. It definitely wasn't the reaction I would have thought any attracted male, human or fey, would give.

Putting a smile on my face, I let him go and moved around the island to take my seat.

"She'd like that name. Fighting meatballs. They're good. I think you're going to love them."

He stuck the red spoon into the dish and joined me. I scooped a portion onto my plate and heard Scath slide his closer.

"My arms are too tired from stirring the noodles. You'll need to serve me, too," he said with an exaggerated sigh.

I smirked and dished him up two helpings. "How's that?"

"Perfect. I like when you serve me."

I snorted even as images I didn't expect flashed in my head. Me on my knees, and him stroking my cheek. My middle gave an unexpected jump.

Clearing my throat, I focused on my own plate. The first

bite distracted me from my runaway thoughts, and I gave a happy groan. His fork clinked on his plate.

"You can cook for me any time," I said after I swallowed. "This is so good."

"Very good," he agreed.

"So, what do you usually do during the day? I'm guessing watching movies yesterday wasn't your normal thing."

"I helped with the food line."

"But that's only been going on for a few days. What about before that?"

"Sometimes, I go on supply runs. Sometimes, I watch feight club."

When he'd mentioned the feight club while on our tour, I'd at first thought it was an actual club with music and drinks. But it wasn't. Apparently, a group of the already-taken ladies got together every day to hone their fighting skills. Archery, hand-to-hand combat, and how to use a knife. It all revolved around defending and killing an infected, and the fey liked to watch and throw out pointers. I respected their determination to ensure they weren't helpless damsels in distress but knew their club wouldn't be my thing even if I could see. So, I'd declined to swing by.

"And in the evening, when all that's done?" I asked.

Silence answered my question, and I didn't think it was because he didn't want to tell me. There wasn't anything to tell. Other people had noticed how the fey roamed around Tenacity now that they could openly come and go as they pleased. The fey didn't have anything to do.

I thought of how they'd taken over guard duty and gathering supplies for a short time when they'd first arrived at Whiteman. It had seemed like a rescue in a way. After all, the fey could fight the infected without dying and had the power to kill hellhounds. But then everything had fallen apart. Mistrust and resentment had created division and had driven the fey to leave Whiteman and establish a place of their own.

Without them, Whiteman had crumbled.

And without us, the fey seemed to have no purpose.

"Well, we'll just need to come up with something then," I said, reaching out to pat his leg.

I overshot my mark and patted his inner thigh.

He tensed.

"Sorry," I said quickly. "No aim without my contacts."

"Where are your contacts?" he asked.

"Probably under a few tons of rubble. I lived in the city before it was bombed," I explained.

"There are contacts and glasses in the supply shed."

"What? Are you serious?"

"Yes. We found some, and Ryan said it would be good to keep them in case they're needed."

"Yes, they're needed. Shit, I wish I had known when we were there." I started shoveling my food into my mouth.

"Would you like to go back and look at the contacts?"

I couldn't answer because my mouth was so full, but I didn't want to look at the contacts. Most likely, they couldn't help me. I needed hard lenses. But some of the glasses might make it possible to see more than just vague blurs. Just the chance to improve my vision even a little was all the motivation I needed to finish off my plate in minutes.

"I'm ready," I said, collecting my plate. "I'll wash the dishes when we get back."

His hands closed over my shoulders and held me in place.

"Leave it here. We will take care of that when we return."

He didn't need to tell me twice. I abandoned my plate and hurried to the door, hand outstretched to ensure I didn't run into a wall in my rush.

"Slow down, Apryl," Scath said when I jammed my foot into my boot. "The glasses are not going anywhere."

"Says the guy who can probably see for miles. I can't see more than a few inches from my face. I don't even have any idea what you look like. Do you know how frustrating that is? If there's a set of glasses that can even help a little, I'll take it."

I jammed my other boot on and grabbed my jacket as I started for the door. Scath caught me by the back of my shirt and turned me around. When I made an impatient sound, the blurry grey orb that was his head shifted to the side.

"It's too cold for you to go without a jacket. Put it on, and I'll carry you to the shed as fast as I can."

I threaded my arms through the sleeves and assumed the "carry me" pose. Instead of picking me up, he zipped my jacket. I made a face, and something brushed my cheek.

"It is not easy to have patience when you want something so badly, is it?"

The empathy in this tone had me wondering what he'd wanted so badly that he understood. Probably a female of his own, which was why he'd jumped at the chance to take me after Fallor declined. And maybe if I found some glasses that worked, I wouldn't be so terrified of not having anywhere to go, and Scath would be free to find someone he was more attracted to.

Smiling, I stood on my toes and brushed his cheek with a kiss.

"Thanks for understanding," I said. "Now, can we go?"

Without another word, he scooped me into his arms and took off out the door. The speed with which he moved robbed me of breath, and I turned my face toward his chest. A few seconds later, he slowed.

"We are here," he said, putting me down. "Are you ready to look at the glasses?"

He held my hand and led me inside to the back corner of a room. There, he grabbed a tote off the top rack.

"This one is filled with glasses," he said as he set it on the floor and removed the lid.

I knelt beside it, lightly running my hand over all the loose glasses. My finger brushed over a bit of paper, and I plucked the frames from the bin to bring them up to my face. The shape of a tag swam into view with letters too small to make out.

"Do all the glasses in this tote have tags?" I asked, hoping I was wrong.

"Yes."

Frustration hit me like a wrecking ball.

"These are display glasses, then. They won't do me any good because the lenses are fake. They don't correct vision."

I listened to the frames clatter and saw him moving.

"What are you doing?"

"I will check them all for tags. Do you want to look at the contacts to see if they are fake too?"

"The contacts probably won't work for me. I needed hard contacts to correct my vision, and I'm guessing the kind here are the soft ones."

I sat on my heels and listened to him methodically sort through the glasses. After several minutes, he sighed, showing a level of frustration that really made me want to hug him. He may not be sexually attracted to me, but he still cared, and that meant everything.

"It's okay," I said. "It was a long shot."

"I don't understand what you mean."

"It's an expression used when people understand that there was a very small chance of things working out. Prescription glasses are made with custom lenses that work for the individual person. So my glasses probably won't work for someone else who needs glasses. And the same goes for theirs working for me. I knew it wouldn't be perfect, but any help visually is better than nothing."

"What happened to your custom glasses?"

"I lost them in the last Whiteman breach. Somewhere between the tents and the main building." I recalled the residual panic that had blanketed the base after that. No one had wanted to leave the main building with the fence down. There'd been so much fear, anger, and blame that I'd just kept my mouth shut about losing my glasses.

"Come," Scath said. "Let's go home. You can have a brownie. Mya says that chocolate makes everything feel better."

"Mya's pretty smart."

CHAPTER SIXTEEN

SCATH

APRYL ATE HER BROWNIE IN SILENCE, AND I KNEW THE DESSERT wasn't going to fix her disappointment. I was torn between wanting to find her glasses at Whiteman and staying with her. Staying won since she still questioned her place with me, and I didn't want her asking any of my brothers if she could live with them.

"Should we watch another movie and then make the fight meatballs?" I asked.

She gave me a soft smile.

"Sure. That sounds like a good idea."

The movie was one of my favorites, but I could tell from Apryl's expression that she wasn't really listening to it. Instead of leaning against me like the day before, she sat straight with her back against the couch and her unfocused gaze aimed at the wall rather than the TV.

However, she seemed a little better when we started dinner after the movie ended. She talked about her grandma and told me about the family she had. Before the earthquakes, she had lived by herself in an apartment, away from her family. So she didn't know if any of them were still alive. She only knew that they weren't at Whiteman.

The sadness in her voice said she already thought they were gone. I gave her another brownie to help her feel better, but it worked as well as the last one.

Her smile returned when I tried rolling the first ball of meat. My large hands created misshapen lumps. Her smaller ones skillfully palmed the meat, coaxing it into a perfect sphere with a nudge of her palm here and a caress of her fingers there.

My balls tingled, and my cock ached by the time she finished. I placed dinner in the oven and excused myself to use the bathroom. Once again, I imagined it was her hands on me and released swiftly.

When I returned to the living room, I found Apryl peering at the books beside the television.

"This is a nice collection," she said. "It looks like all romance."

"Do you want to read?" I asked, already imagining the possibilities.

She shook her head and set the book down again.

"I'd probably give myself a headache in a few minutes. Too much eye strain without my glasses."

"Do you think they're still there?" I asked.

"At Whiteman? Probably somewhere under the snow." Her expression turned hopeful. "Are you thinking of looking for them?"

"Yes, but I don't want to leave you alone."

"I'll be fine alone. I swear."

I glanced at the oven and at the window. I had less than an hour of daylight left.

"I'll go look, but only if you allow someone to stay with you."

"I don't need a babysitter."

I debated how much to say as I gently clasped her arms.

"You are not dead weight. You are smart and capable. But if another breach happened, would you be able to see the difference between an infected human and a normal one?"

She glanced away from me.

"Now that you're here, I don't want to risk you. Even a cut or a burn would be too much. Please allow someone to stay with you while I'm gone."

She nodded, still looking sad.

I nudged her chin so she would look up at me again.

"I will find your glasses. I promise."

Some of her sadness disappeared, and she smiled at me. The tenderness in her eyes burrowed deep into my chest and wrapped around my heart. That was the look I'd wanted from her. Yet, I struggled to breathe now. I wanted to dip my head and taste her lips. Or pull her into my arms and hold her the way Tor held June.

Instead, I said, "Be here when I return."

Before I could stop myself, I gave in to the urge and pressed my forehead to hers. Her smile grew, and she gently set her palm against my cheek.

"I will. I promise."

Knowing daylight was fading fast, I retreated. And with one last look at Apryl, I headed for the door. I didn't want to go. I feared she would search for another fey to stay with, instead of me. But I saw how much finding her glasses would mean to her, and I wanted to be the one to give her that joy.

I didn't think I would see Fallor approaching my house as I closed the door behind me.

"What are you doing here?" I asked.

"There are females searching for homes in Tenacity but are

not being welcomed like Apryl. I thought you would want to know before I told the others."

"I am happy with Apryl."

"But is she happy with you?"

I glanced at the melting snow on my sidewalk.

"It takes females time to find their happiness. Hannah took weeks."

"Hannah is different from most females. Is Apryl happy?"

"She still fears I will find another female I will want more than I want her. Until she understands she has a home here and does not need to do the things she said to earn it, I doubt she will be happy. She needs time," I repeated.

Fallor nodded.

"That is true. Is that why you are leaving?"

"No. Apryl cannot see well. She lost her glasses during the last Whiteman breach. I'm going to go look for them."

"I'll go with you."

"We will need more help and someone to stay with Apryl. Dinner is in the oven, and I don't want her to burn herself because she can't see well."

"If there is food, Brooke will stay with her."

We jogged to Brooke's house and waited for Solin to answer the door. When he invited us in, I frowned at the scent of cooking meat.

"Are you making dinner?" I asked.

"My amazing husband sure is," Brooke called. "There is enough if you want to join us."

Solin shook his head slightly.

"Babe," she said, "I can see you. It doesn't matter if they stay or go. My vagina is on break until tomorrow."

I grinned at Solin's frustration and disappointment.

"Perhaps you would like to meet Scath's new female then?" Fallor called.

I heard a chair scrape against tile, and Brooke appeared beside Solin.

"You have a girl?" she asked, looking at me. "What's her name? When did she get here? How serious are things?"

I liked Brooke. She wasn't afraid of the fey and answered questions like Angel did...when Solin wasn't keeping her in the bedroom.

"Her name is Apryl. She asked to live with me yesterday. We are not having sex yet, but she is mine. She cannot see well without her glasses. Will you stay with her while I look for them? We made her grandmother's fighting meatballs for dinner."

"Absolutely, yes. You know I won't turn down a cooked meal." She patted Solin's arm and smiled up at him. "We can bring along what you've made too."

"Thank you, Brooke," I said.

Fallor and I hurried away from their house. By the time we reached the wall, four of our brothers had joined us. Cheri had asked Farco for some "me-time," which meant he couldn't return home until after dark. So he was willing to help. And Terri had asked Groth to leave for a while. He said Terri enjoyed sex more when he wasn't home to hear her pleasure. Eitri was just interested in helping so he could look for things to impress Danielle. And Bauts had nothing else to do.

The six of us cleared Tolerance's walls and ran toward Whiteman. It didn't take long to reach the mangled gates, but it did steal precious time in the light.

Once we reached the hangar, we spread out and walked the path to the tents several times. The dusting of snow on the ground made it easy to see where we'd been but hard to see any glasses. We moved carefully in the fading light.

I was on the third pass in my section when I heard Bauts

call out. An infected echoed the sound nearby. Ignoring it, I jogged toward Bauts.

He stood in an area not far from the first row of tents, holding something in his hands. When he heard me approach, he looked up, his expression twisted with regret.

"They were well hidden under the snow," he said, holding out the glasses.

They didn't look like the ones in the storage shed. The lenses were thick. Thick enough that they hadn't broken under Bauts' foot. However, the frames were not so lucky. The plastic had snapped in several places, leaving the glasses in three pieces with the lenses separate.

"I am sorry, Scath," he said.

"There are many frames in the shed. Apryl will find new ones." I clasped his arm. "Thank you for finding them."

Another infected moaned nearby.

"Let us clear the infected and return." I tucked the pieces into the pocket of my pants, and we went to find the others.

CHAPTER SEVENTEEN

APRYL

BROOKE HUMMED AS SHE ATE THE MEATBALL.

"This is so good. Thanks for having us over."

I smiled slightly, glad Scath had sent nice people to stay with me. After knocking on the door and letting herself in, Brooke had made herself at home like she was my long-lost friend. And she felt like it too. She was easy to talk to and funny. But most importantly, she hadn't batted an eye at the fact that I couldn't see.

"Thanks for taking them out of the oven," I said. "I probably would have overcooked them on my own."

"Will you teach me how to make these?" Solin asked.

He sat at the table with us. Up until then, he'd been quietly eating and listening to our conversation.

"Sure," I said. "I'm glad you like them."

"The fey are big on the meat-eating," Brooke said. "They don't mind steaks and whatnot, but they hate when we start mixing stuff into the meat."

"Except like this," he said.

I smiled a little wider at the praise and ate my last half meatball while wondering how Scath's search was going.

The sky was already dark outside, and there was no sign of him yet. I knew not to worry, though. He could handle himself out there in ways I wouldn't ever be able to manage. But it did feel weird being in the house after dark without him.

"Would you care for some brownies?" I asked. "We made some earlier."

"Yes, please," Brooke said, already getting up. "Tell me where they are, and I'll serve you since you're letting me eat your food."

Solin started gathering our dishes.

"Do you think they'll find your glasses?" Brooke asked as she moved around the kitchen.

"I hope so. I'm tired of not being able to see anything. I mean, they won't be as good as my contacts, but they're better than nothing, you know?"

"I honestly can't imagine. How did you survive this long?" She didn't say it with any hint of judgment. Just awe and a helping of empathy.

"Well, I kept it a secret as best I could once we came here to Tolerance. Everyone was so angry and scared that they didn't pay much attention to the fact that I stayed in my room all the time. When the breach happened, I locked myself in the closet. One of the fey found me while doing a sweep of the houses for infected and led me to where everyone was gathering by the wall. But it was chaos still with people splitting up. I kept my head down and followed the majority until I found myself in a new house in Tenacity with a bunch of strangers. And, well…" I shrugged. "I just kept hiding by staying in my room and out of the way.

"The few times guilt got the better of me and I tried to help, it always went wrong. I broke things, hurt myself, and wasted supplies. My housemates preferred it when I stayed in my room. But when Matt and June announced the restructuring and mandatory pitching in with no exceptions, I knew I was screwed."

Brooke set a plate in front of me and gave my arm a consoling squeeze.

"I'm sorry you went through all of that. I promise that it's not like that over here."

I didn't say anything because it sort of did feel like it was the same here. Fallor had changed his mind within hours of taking me in, and I still feared that he'd deliver some other female that Scath would like better than me.

The bite of brownie didn't drown my feelings as I'd hoped, but it sure was good.

Before I could swallow, the door opened.

"Hey, Scath and Fallor," Brooke said.

I stood in a hurry and turned toward the fey. They both looked pretty much the same with blurry grey blobs for their heads outlined by long black hair. Scath had a blue blur for a torso when he'd left, but both were matching grey blurs now.

"Um," I said, my gaze flicking between the two. "You have to tell me who is who. I can't tell. And where did your shirts go?"

They stopped.

"Whatever you just said has Scath looking really happy," Brooke said. "Is it because she noticed you didn't have a shirt on?"

"No," Scath said. "Apryl, when you were looking for a new place to live yesterday, did Fallor offer you a room?"

"Yeah…you already know he did. You were there."

One of them grunted.

"I was there," Scath said. "*I* was the one who asked you to live with me, not Fallor. When I returned, you weren't there, so

I asked Fallor to watch for you while I checked for you at the meeting."

My mouth dropped open, and my gaze shifted between the two. I hadn't been paying attention when the guy offered me the room. Not to his clothes. Not to his voice. Nothing. I'd been too excited that I'd found a place to stay.

But hadn't I noticed he'd sounded different? Yet, I hadn't stopped to ask questions.

My face started to heat.

"I kissed Fallor," I whispered, mortified.

"Yes," Scath said. "Because you thought he was me."

I covered my face with my hands. "I'm so sorry."

Fingers plucked mine away until I was looking up at Scath.

"You couldn't see. I understand. Fallor understands." He continued tugging my hand away and set something in it.

"These are the only glasses we found."

I used my other hand to feel what he'd given me, which was a mess of pieces. It had been crazy to hope that they'd survived unscathed, but I had. And now, here they were, busted beyond repair into several pieces.

"That doesn't look good," Brooke said. "Want me to see if I can tape the frames together?"

I shook my head. "There's no point. I can feel it cracked around the lens frame. It won't hold the lenses in."

"You can choose new frames," Scath said.

"Sure," I agreed, even though I knew it wasn't that easy.

Picking up a lens, I brought it to my eye to see if it was as damaged as the frame. It appeared dirty but unbroken. Looking through it, a body swam into partial focus. I could see abs. Sweet mother of God, could I see abs. Chiseled hard ridges.

I lifted my gaze and blinked at Scath. His grey skin wasn't a shock to me, but the details were. Hearing about pointed ears and unusual eyes was completely different from seeing them.

His green gaze held mine, but I barely noticed the vertical pupil as I studied his handsome face. Cleft chin. Strong jaw. Kissable lips.

"Whoa," I breathed and glanced at Brooke. "Am I really seeing an Adonis?"

She chuckled. "Yep. And that's our cue to go." She hugged me quickly. "Have fun with your new glasses."

My gaze shifted to the fey who stood behind Scath as Brooke and Solin left.

"I'm really embarrassed about the mix-up," I said. "I don't normally go around kissing people."

"I understand," Fallor said.

"You don't have a wife or girlfriend I need to apologize to, do you?"

"No," he said. "I will go too. Have a good night."

I focused on Scath as the door closed. It was incredible to finally see some detail. He watched me as I studied him, and I wished I had frames to hold the lenses in place so my hands would be free to do some exploring.

"Will you be able to see the difference between us with that piece of glass?" he asked.

"It's a little blurry when you're farther away, but I'd be able to tell the difference when you're close like this."

"Will using both pieces make your vision clearer?"

"A little more, yes. But it's limited in how much clearer. My contacts almost had my vision to 20/60, which is pretty good. Like twice as good as it is now."

He grunted, and we continued to study each other. The man was positively mouthwatering, like those first responder calendars I used to buy. For charity. Because I'm a good person.

"Are you going to tell me where your shirt went?" I asked.

"There were infected at Whiteman. We removed them before we left."

I tipped my head up to look at his face again and noticed his hair was still wet.

"I heard killing infected is messy business," I said. "That you tear off their heads."

"It is."

"Kind of glad I haven't witnessed that. I'm glad you weren't hurt. And thank you for finding these."

"Do you want me to go to the supply shed for the frames?" he asked.

"I'm not sure they'll work. See how thick my lenses are?" I opened my hand with the other lens. "And there's a groove cut around it? That groove has to fit into the frames just right. And there are different sizes and shapes of frames. I'm not saying we won't find one that works, but it probably won't be easy. And we'll probably break a few frames trying."

"Then we will find more," he said.

"Okay. I guess we don't have anything else to do before bed, do we?"

He grunted and turned toward the door before pausing. "I'm not running away."

"I know you're not. And I'm really sorry that I kissed someone else in front of you. That kiss was meant for you."

Thanks to my lens, I didn't miss the sadness that washed over his expression.

"I don't want your fear kisses or your trade sex, Apryl."

"Then what do you want?" I asked, needing to hear it.

"I want whatever is real." He started for the door and said, "I'll be back in a few minutes," just before leaving me alone.

Heaving a sigh, I set the pieces of my glasses on the counter and thought back to the mess of mistakes I'd made over the last couple of days because of that initial misunderstanding. But now that I understood he wanted the real deal, could I give it to him?

Thoughts churning, I made my way back to the bathroom. I was overdue for a shower and some serious thinking time.

CHAPTER EIGHTEEN

SCATH

MY HEART WAS FULL, AND I GRINNED THE WHOLE WAY TO THE storage shed. Apryl hadn't meant to kiss Fallor. She didn't prefer him over me.

I knew her disinterest in Fallor didn't change that she still thought she needed to trade sex for food and a home. But it did mean that her heart wasn't already claimed by another and was free to be claimed by me.

And I'd already started my slow assault with her glasses.

The way her eyes had lit with excitement when she'd looked through them the first time proved I'd done something meaningful for her. Now, I needed to find her frames that would work.

Moving through the aisles of supplies, I made my way to the tote. The door opened in the living room, and I carried out the tote to see Drav looking at the supply shelves.

"How is Mya?" I asked. "Another headache?"

"Yes. She said that it's stress, and she wants more chocolate."

"Stress? Does she worry about the baby?"

"No. She worries about her brother. He, Eden, and Shelby, a new female, went to look for places like this one. A hound was discovered, and a few of our brothers were injured. They will live, but Mya does not like any injuries."

I nodded, understanding. "Apryl and I made brownies. You're welcome to take ours, so you don't need to make anything."

He grunted and headed for the door with me.

"Is it hard?" I asked. "Watching her suffer to give you a baby?"

"Very," he said, jogging beside me as we left.

"Do you regret it?"

Drav sighed. "Every time she hurts, yes. But when the baby kicks under my hand, I regret nothing."

"I want children, but I don't want Apryl to suffer."

"Mom says every pregnancy is different. Angel doesn't suffer as Mya does."

"Angel's baby is human," I said.

Drav grunted and waited for me to open the front door. The shower was running in the back bedroom.

I put the tote on the counter so Apryl would be able to see it. Drav waited as I removed the brownies from the refrigerator.

"Here. I hope Mya feels better quickly."

"Thank you."

Drav left with the brownies, and I headed for the bedroom. The water turned off as I approached.

"I'm back," I said through the bathroom door. "I'll wait for you in the kitchen."

"Wait," she called as I was about to turn away.

The door flew open, and I stared at Apryl. She had her hair wrapped in a smaller towel and a larger one around her body.

Water ran down her chest, disappearing in the crack between her breasts. And with each step she took toward me, the beautiful curve of her hip peeked out.

I inhaled her scent as she drew closer.

"I have something I need to say to you," she said.

I waited.

"Your home is perfect for me, and I'm grateful for all the food you have. But that's not why I'm staying. Before I could see you, I liked the sound of your voice. I still like it, but I like the way you take care of me while letting me do things for myself even more. And now that I can see you, I think you're very handsome, Scath."

She wasn't holding up a lens to her eye as she spoke, but her gaze still moved over my features as she set her hand on my chest. Her feather-light touch sent a shiver of need through me.

"Why are you telling me this?" I asked.

"I didn't mean to kiss Fallor. I meant to kiss you. And the next time I try, I want you to know I'm doing it because I'm attracted to you, not to pay you back for the roof over my head or the food in my belly."

I'd yearned to hear those words from her and wanted to believe them, but I found it difficult to believe she had changed how she viewed things in the time it took me to retrieve the frames. She'd mistaken Fallor for me because she couldn't see and had admitted the single lens made things clearer but not perfect. Would she still find me handsome when using both lenses? Would she still be interested in me if she knew she could live with any male of her choosing? That they would all willingly provide for her just for her company, not for her body?

"You doubt it," she said, not sounding too upset. "That's

okay. I'd doubt it, too, if I were in your shoes. I'm just asking you to give me some time to prove it."

I frowned at her choice of words.

"Do you still believe that I will change my mind and ask you to leave?" I asked.

Her expression changed to one filled with guilt.

"We both know I'm not your ideal girl. Fallor will probably show up with someone you can actually leave alone with a hot oven and not have to worry about her. But thanks to the glasses you found, I won't be helpless."

I didn't know how else to reassure her other than to admit the truth.

"Fallor has already returned with word of other women looking for homes."

Shock and hurt showed on her face, and I quickly clasped her arms as her hand fell from my chest.

"There are many of us and very few willing females. Why would I send away the one I have? One who thinks I'm handsome and touches me freely?

"I want you to stay here, Apryl, but I want you to stay here because there is nowhere else you would rather be. Not because you think there is nowhere else for you to go." I took a steadying breath. "It doesn't matter that you cannot cook or could accidentally hurt yourself if you are left alone...any of my brothers would gladly have you if you do not want to remain with me."

Her gaze flicked over mine, and I saw the uncertainty there. It tore at my heart, and I forced myself to release her. But I couldn't help the way my fingers caressed down her bare arms.

"Will you stay with me, Apryl?" I asked.

"Wait. Let me get this straight. You're telling me all the

other single fey would jump at a chance to take me in just to prove that you really want me to stay with you?"

"Yes."

She looked down, hiding whatever emotions she might be feeling from my gaze.

"I know what you want," she said. "I know what all the fey want. You want forever and babies. It's hard to think of forever when I'm still trying to figure out how I survived this long. And as for babies, can you imagine having a toddler as blind as I am? I don't want to bring babies into this world just to watch them die.

"So I guess whether or not I stay is still up to you and if you're okay being with a woman who is struggling with the idea of a long-term relationship and having babies when it feels like the world is still slowly dying."

She looked up at me then, showing me all the vulnerability she was feeling, and I felt the same. This woman needed more than a male who could provide for her. She needed a male who would take the time to understand her fears and insecurities. And after living with the humans for so many months, I knew understanding her fears didn't mean overcoming them.

I wanted children as badly as the rest of my brothers. But badly enough to give up Apryl?

Seeing her had made me yearn for a baby with her brown skin and pretty eyes. If I couldn't have that, would I find anything else as satisfying? No. My heart said Apryl was meant to be mine. And if that meant no children, so be it.

"I want you to stay," I repeated. "And we will build a long-term relationship slowly, starting with trust. Please trust me when I say I want *you* to be here."

"I'll try," she said.

"Good. Get dressed and come to the kitchen. We will fix your glasses so you can see with both lenses at once."

"Okay." She started to turn away and paused. "Thank you, Scath."

I wasn't prepared for her sudden and almost violent hug. Her arms wrapped around my waist with the force of one of my brothers as she squeezed me. And it incited that same need to prove my dominance but in a completely different way.

The weight of her breasts teased my torso as wickedly as her freshly washed scent. Inhaling deeply, I caged her against me, skimming my palms over her damp shoulders. I wanted her under me, rubbing herself against me. I wanted it so badly that my cock throbbed in time with her racing pulse.

Slow, I reminded myself.

Fighting the need to pick her up and carry her to the bedroom, I gripped her shoulder and gently pried her away from me. She seemed reluctant to let go, which only fed my aching need for her. When she finally did release her hold, she looked up at me with her beautiful brown eyes and…

Her towel came loose and dropped to the floor.

Her mouth fell open, and I stared. At everything. Her deliciously rounded breasts. The soft swell of her midsection. The very oddly trimmed remains of the tuft of hair that covered her pussy. Then back up to those invitingly parted lips. On her mouth.

Swallowing a growl, I cupped the back of her head and struggled to rein in the intense desire to taste the lips of the woman who gave my life purpose.

"I'm sorry. I didn't mean for that to happen," she said, her panicked gaze flicking to my mouth.

Was she thinking of kissing me? I wanted to groan and lean in to encourage her. Instead, I forced my stiff fingers to relax against the back of her head. Hadn't I promised to move slowly after she'd admitted her fears to me? She needed my understanding, and I needed her trust. Pushing her wouldn't get either of us those things.

"I will wait for you in the kitchen," I said.

It took everything in me to turn away and leave her.

CHAPTER NINETEEN

APRYL

I DIDN'T KNOW WHAT TO THINK AS SCATH LEFT THE ROOM.

He'd said several times that he wanted me, but when my towel had fallen off—truly a freak accident this time due to my over-exuberant hug—he hadn't even batted an eye. Even with my tits out with nipples blazing.

No, not true. He'd kind of grabbed the back of my head as if I was some "cute," misguided child.

What straight man didn't try to cop a feel? Or look?

Frowning, I wondered if maybe I'd missed an eye-groping. I'd been looking at him, but his lighter eyes made it kind of hard to tell where he was looking. Yet, *if* he had looked, it had to have been brief. Men who were interested didn't glance. They stared. They appreciated the view. Why would he want a woman he wasn't into enough to do that?

He'd said it himself…there were a lot of them and not very many females who were willing. So, he could be desperate enough for one that he would take one he wasn't attracted to.

I made a face at the thought and went to the closet, wondering if I could be with someone who wasn't attracted to me. Grabbing a thong, I started to get dressed and acknowledged that mutual attraction was a must for me. Without it, I'd always doubt how long-term our relationship would be. If what we had could even be called a relationship.

No sex. No affection. Just cohabitating?

His insistence that I stay just didn't make any sense to me. Why else keep me if not for sex? It wasn't like I brought any other useful skills to the table. I couldn't cook or clean well and didn't want to spawn the next generation of apocalyptic snack food for the infected.

I tugged a shirt on over my head, skipping a bra, and struggled to think of even one reason Scath wouldn't ditch me the moment someone willing to have his babies came along. There wasn't one, which meant there was zero point in staying long-term.

That didn't mean I needed to pack up and leave, though. As he'd said, he wanted me to be here…for now. So I had some time. Based on how reluctant the women in Tenacity were, I probably had a few weeks at least. Plenty of time to figure out how to fix my glasses, gain a useful skill or two, and find a fey who was interested in me.

Pretending to feel better about my situation, I pulled on a clean pair of shorts and went to join Scath in the kitchen.

He had the tote open on the counter and was lining up all the frames in neat rows. When he heard my approach, he looked up but quickly focused on the glasses again.

"I saved you some of the meatballs we made," I said, walking around the counter and picking up a lens to see what I was doing. "Are you hungry?"

"Yes."

The almost pained word had me pausing and glancing his way. His head was bent as he sorted through the frames.

"Are you okay?" I asked.

"Frustrated," he said. He held up a narrow set of frames. "I'm not sure any of these will work for you."

I smiled sadly, wishing he was attracted to me. The men I'd dated in the past hadn't cared about the little things as much as Scath did. They'd never understood that all those little ways of showing a woman they cared added up to something big. Something heart-rending and addictive.

"I kind of figured it wouldn't be easy," I said. "But we'll figure something out. It's better to have lenses without a frame than no lenses at all."

He grunted and went back to sorting as I warmed up his dinner. When it was ready, I slid it in front of him along with a fork and moved the tote to the floor while he took his first bite.

I grinned at his groan and straightened from my bent-over position.

"Good, right?" I asked.

"Yes."

"Grandma knew what she was doing," I said. "She didn't like all the recipes with ketchup and barbeque sauce, so she made her own. The secret is in the vinegar and molasses."

I went to look over the frames he'd set aside. There were a few potential options that looked like they could support my thicker lenses. I tried test-fitting the lens, but the frames were just the wrong shape.

"When I was fitted for glasses, they had a machine that would warm up the earpiece so they could bend it to fit behind my ears. I wonder if we can get the lens to fit by putting the frame in some really hot water."

He immediately left his seat and filled a pot with water. While we waited for it to boil, he finished his meal.

"Let's take a set of frames that don't look that promising and see if the water even works to reshape them," I said.

We let them sit in the water for a minute before trying.

They had a little give but not a lot. We cracked five sets of frames before I called it quits.

"I don't think this is going to work," I said. "The frames just aren't the right shape."

He turned over the frames and looked at the lenses for several beats.

"I think I have another idea, but we'll need Dad's help." He glanced at the windows. "It's too late to ask him now. But we can go see him in the morning."

"Dad? Who's he?"

"Mya's father. He knows many ways of making things. I think with his tools, we can carve this piece from wood and attach any of these plastic arms."

I grinned at the flutter of hope blooming in my chest. "That could work."

Scath grunted and started putting away the undamaged frames. I glanced at the clock on the stove. Brooke had set it for me, using the time from her watch, which she thought was fairly accurate. It was only eight.

"Do you want to watch a movie?" I asked.

"It would be better if we slept. Making your frames will take time, and I would like to start at first light."

"Oh, yeah. Sure." I took his plate to the sink and started washing it. When I turned around to see if he was ready to go to bed, he was already putting a pillow and a folded blanket on the couch.

"Do you need anything before you go to bed?" he asked, not looking my way.

"No. I guess not."

Trying not to overthink the situation, I went to the bedroom. However, my confusion ate at me as I brushed my teeth and got ready for bed. Why keep me if he had zero use for me? Why talk about a long-term relationship if he was going to sleep on the couch? Sure, he said we'd take it slow, but what exactly were we taking slow? Getting to know one another? Because that was what it felt like.

Maybe sleeping in the same bed was a bigger deal to him than it was to me.

What did it matter if he slept out there, though? Hadn't I already decided that I was going to go out there and find someone new once I had my glasses fixed? Tomorrow would be a perfect opportunity to start meeting people.

But the idea of trying to meet someone else while Scath worked on custom frames for me made me uncomfortable. Like I was using him just to get the frames so I could see again and then bail.

I slid under the covers but only stayed there for a few seconds.

The light was off in the living room as I made my way down the dark hallway, but I heard him sit up.

"Is something wrong?" he asked.

"Yeah. A lot, actually."

I heard him get up and hurry toward me.

"Are you hurt?" he asked, his voice laced with concern.

His hand skimmed over my arm like he was checking for injuries. That level of caring made my heart skip a beat.

"No. I'm confused, Scath. You said you want a long-term relationship, and I get that you want to take things slow, but I don't understand why you'd want to sleep on the couch instead of in the bed with me. Isn't the point of going slow to get to know each other? We're not talking much. We're spending some time together, but it feels—" I sighed. "—I don't know. Stilted, I guess. I'm just trying to figure out why you want me here when you're so obviously not attracted to me."

His hand left my arm. Silence echoed around me.

Frowning, I lifted my free hand to feel in front of me. Fingers caught mine.

"I am here," Scath said softly.

"Are you? Because it doesn't feel like it sometimes. What do you want from me, Scath? Why did you offer to let me live with you and mention a long-term relationship? Is this really the kind of relationship you want? Distant? Separate?"

CHAPTER TWENTY

SCATH

I LOOKED AT HER BEAUTIFUL, UPTURNED FACE AND FOUGHT THE urge to fit my lips to hers and take what I knew she would willingly give. But I couldn't. A kiss wasn't all I wanted. I wanted Apryl. I wanted her so badly I could think of little else but the scent of her skin and the soft pillow of her lips.

Yet, if I told her how badly I wanted her, would she understand it wasn't only for sex? Would she know that I wanted *her*, the woman who fascinated me with every little smile and graceful stretch of her fingers? With every cautious step and inquisitive question?

My fingers played with hers as I considered my next words.

"Did you know that my brothers and I lived in caves deep beneath the surface before we came here?" I asked.

"Yeah. I know that."

"There was no sky. Only the blackness of the caves or the dim glow of the crystals.

"The first time I saw the sunlit sky, it hurt my eyes. I could barely keep them open, but even as they watered, I couldn't stop looking at the sky. It was strange, yes, but so beautiful. So unlike anything I could have imagined. And now that I've seen it and felt the sun's warmth on my face, I never want to return to the caves, no matter how much I might miss the home I knew.

"And it was like that when my brothers and I first saw females. They were strange but so beautiful.

"When I look at you, Apryl, it is like looking at the bright sky for the first time. But it is not my eyes that hurt."

I pressed her palm to my bare chest, right over my heart.

"The thought that you might not want me as I want you pains me here, and I struggle to find the words that will win your heart. I don't know how else to prove my attraction to you."

She slowly shook her head at me. "Show some interest in me—especially when I'm naked. Sleep next to me at night. Touch me. Kiss me. Any form of physical contact, really."

My cock ached at the thought of touching and kissing her.

With a sigh, I set my forehead to hers. The way her pupils remained unfocused told me that she couldn't see me. But I could see everything about her. Including the way her thin shirt clearly displayed her enticingly dark nipples.

"I wish to know your mind before I know your body," I said hoarsely.

"Can't you get to know both at the same time?"

"Until I know your mind, how will I know if you are offering your body because you fear losing your home rather than because you desire me more than any other male in existence?"

She frowned slightly as a small smile tugged at her lips. It was an odd combination I'd never witnessed before.

"In existence?" she said. "That's a pretty tall order. But I guess that makes sense. Why settle for someone who isn't fully committed to being with you, right? Okay. Then we'll work on getting to know each other. But can you please commit to sleeping in the same bed as me? We don't have to do anything physical. I just like knowing that you're there. And we can talk as we're winding down from the day."

Unable to help myself, I pulled back to smooth my fingers over the soft curve of her cheek.

"Yes. I will sleep beside you."

"Every night," she said, wearing a determined look on her face.

"Every night," I echoed.

She flashed another smile and, holding my hand, led me down the hall to the bedroom. I watched her slide under the covers and tilt her head as she listened for me to join her. If the sun had blinded me that first day on the surface, seeing Apryl bathed in the light from the sliver of moon struck me dumb.

I wanted to tell her how much I ached for her. How much I wanted her touches and kisses. Instead, I got into bed with her and lay beside her, not daring to touch her.

"Has Dad made frames for glasses before?" she asked.

"I don't know."

"Why do you think he can help, then?"

"He will know what tools to use to do what I wish."

She rolled toward me, tucking her arm under her head.

"I've gotten used to fumbling my way through one day to the next," she said. "But I really want to be able to see you."

Her words filled me with hope and desire.

"Why?"

"So I can see your eyes when you're looking at me."

That worried me. Most humans didn't find our eyes attractive. What if she saw them and changed her mind about living with me?

She closed her eyes and moved a little closer so I could feel each of her exhales on my bare chest. I leaned in until my nose almost touched her hair and inhaled her scent.

"I can't remember the last time I felt this safe and warm," she said softly. "Being here with you is addicting. I know you think I might only like you because of the food and the house, but neither of those things would mean anything without you. You're the safety, Scath. Not the house."

Her arm slipped around my waist and settled there as she sighed softly.

"I wasn't kidding when I said I missed contact. I really hope you're the snuggly sort of guy who likes hugs because I'm that kind of girl."

"I like hugs," I said, trying to ignore my reaction to having her in my arms.

"Good."

I waited for more, but she didn't say anything else as her breathing evened out. She didn't roll away from me once she was asleep but melted even closer.

Thoughts clouded by the need throbbing through my shaft, I ran my hand over the length of her arm. Down and up again. My wrist brushed against her breast, and I stilled. Her breathing remained even as my gaze darted to the tempting mound of flesh that had tormented me since she emerged from the bedroom after her shower. Her nipple called to me, begging for a touch, for attention.

Transfixed, I lifted my hand from her arm and brushed a fingertip over the dark circle. She didn't stir as I gently explored the feel of her through the almost non-existent shirt. However, when my palm covered the entirety of her breast and I gave a gentle squeeze, something did happen. Her nipple pebbled under my palm.

Biting back a groan, I released her and rolled onto my back. Her arm slipped lower, settling on my lower stomach. My cock pulsed with need only inches from her fingers. I imagined her hand sliding down and gripping my shaft firmly. Stroking it. Teasing the head. Then her mouth closing over it.

My hips bucked without permission, and I began to release. Each pulse hit me with unexpected force until I finished with a weak grunt. Stunned, I lay there for a moment and tried to catch my breath.

Apryl sighed softly and moved closer to me, resting her head on my chest and pinning me in place. I couldn't decide if I should settle in or get up to shower and change.

The idea of leaving her had me wrapping an arm around her waist and holding her close. Rather than focusing on how she felt pressed against me, I focused on what I would need to do the next day. Dad would know how to cut a thin slice of wood. He may even have an easier way to cut away the excess until we had the general shape of the frame face. The rest I would be able to do with a knife.

I visualized Apryl's reaction when I handed her frames that would hold her lenses and felt my cock stir. Easing out from underneath her, I grabbed a clean pair of shorts and headed to the bathroom.

Two releases later, I felt sufficiently relaxed and joined her in bed. She immediately reclaimed a portion of my chest for her pillow, making dissatisfied sounds until she was curled around me once more.

Smiling to myself and thinking I was the luckiest fey in the world to have found a woman who loved touching, I closed my eyes.

I only managed a few hours of sleep before I woke to an explosion of pain radiating from my groin. Before I could process what was happening, the weight of Apryl's leg shifted off my waist. Already firing more danger signals than my brain could process, my testicles seized a second time despite the less aggressive brush with her knee as she straightened her leg.

The first breath I managed was barely more than a moan. The second came a little easier, and with it, I managed to protectively cover myself and roll away from Apryl, who remained peacefully asleep.

Each step toward the bathroom sent a new shard of pain through my groin. I wasn't entirely sure I would be able to father children or even achieve an erection ever again. But gradually, the throbbing eased, and I could manage a deep inhale with minimal wincing.

Not wanting to go back on my word and sleep on the couch, I decided to start breakfast while I held a snow compress between my legs.

CHAPTER TWENTY-ONE

APRYL

I WOKE WITH A STRETCH AND A HUGE SENSE OF CONTENTMENT, immediately thinking of Scath's words the night before. The guy was crazy if he thought he had no word game because he'd absolutely won me over by comparing me to the sunlit sky.

When he'd followed me to the room, I'd expected some more awkwardness. Especially when I rolled toward him to test the sincerity of his claim to like me. Instead, I'd been surprised by his willingness to let me snuggle up to him and how he'd admitted to liking hugs. It was a good sign. So was how amazing it felt falling asleep in his arms. Granted, he hadn't exactly returned the snuggle, but it was only our second night together, and he had said he wanted to take it slow.

It finally felt like we were off to a decent start, though.

A hint of something delicious teased my nose, and I turned my head to look at the empty spot beside me. I wasn't mad that he hadn't stayed in bed, not when he was out there cooking me breakfast. After everything I'd been through in recent months, it felt damn good to be spoiled. I just wished he'd let me return the favor.

Shaking my head due to my bad luck, which had started all his doubt in the first place, I got out of bed and went to the closet to pick out something new to wear. I skipped the paper-thin options and selected a top with a bit more material since we'd be meeting other people.

Even though I no longer planned to find a fey more interested in me than Scath, I wanted to look presentable. I did not want to make a poor first impression when it came to meeting the parents of the leader of Tolerance.

Dressed in jeans and a long-sleeved shirt, sans bra, I grabbed my lenses from the nightstand and went out to the kitchen. Scath stood at the counter stirring something in a bowl.

"Morning," I said, watching him. "It smells amazing in here. Thanks for starting breakfast."

"You're welcome."

I sat on the stool. "I can't remember the last time I slept so comfortably."

Was it my imagination, or had he just winced?

"How did you sleep?" I asked.

He didn't glance back at me when he answered that he'd slept fine.

Tapping my finger on the counter, I watched him through the lens and tried to decide if he was being standoffish again or if he was really focused on cooking.

"Can I help with anything?" I asked.

"No. Stay where you are. I'm almost done."

He poured some of the batter onto a hot griddle, and while the pancakes cooked, he pulled out several dishes from the oven. He lined the counter with scrambled eggs, hashbrowns, sausages, biscuits and gravy, and a pitcher of orange juice.

"How long, exactly, have you been awake?" I asked, looking at it all.

He reached up and scratched the edge of one of his ears. "I'm not sure."

"Don't fey sleep as long as humans?"

The tips of his ears darkened, and he turned away to flip the pancakes. "Sometimes. Eat. We can leave as soon as we are finished."

His arm brushed my side as he set a plate in front of me and took the stool beside mine. Reassured that he wasn't withdrawing, I helped myself to some of everything.

The first bite of biscuits and gravy drew a long "mmm" from me.

"These biscuits are amazing," I said, already moving on to try some egg with the gravy. "This is so good."

If I offended him by talking around a mouthful of food, he didn't let on. He just kept eating his own breakfast as I wolfed down mine. I didn't manage to finish everything before I leaned back with a groan.

"You're not going to throw this away, right? We can have it again for lunch."

He chuckled. "I won't throw it away, but Mom will probably want to feed us while we're there."

I got up and started helping him clear away the dishes with one hand while watching him through a lens with the other.

"How did you learn to cook like this?" I asked. "I imagine it's not the same food you were used to."

"No, it's very different. Mary and Emily have been teaching some of us how to make human meals so we can help with the food kitchen at Tenacity."

The food kitchen was still relatively new. Less than a week old.

"How long were they teaching you before they started the food kitchen?"

"Two days."

"Wow." I put away the dried plates and turned toward him. "Were you just messing with me about needing help with the brownies, then?"

He shook his head and put the last wrapped dish into the refrigerator.

"No. The boxes can have unique ingredients and measurements for what's needed, which I can't read. The biscuit recipe I know from memory. The same with the pancakes and how to make the eggs."

"Ah. What else do you know how to make?" I asked as we moved toward the door.

"Grandma's fighting meatballs."

The way he grinned a little as he said it sent a thrill through me.

"Thank you for teaching me," he added.

"You're welcome."

He helped me into my jacket and zipped me up before stepping back and studying me.

"Would you like me to carry you there, or would you like to walk?"

I tucked my other lens into my jacket pocket and glanced at the window. It was still really early. Just after dawn.

"I'd like to walk," I said, thinking that Mya's parents might appreciate a little more time before we showed up unannounced.

"So tell me more about Tolerance. I didn't get to know much when I was here last time."

"The homes all have solar, thanks to Dad and Ryan, and wood heat. The wall is being refortified in some places, making it higher for better vantage points to watch for infected and hounds. With the arrival of the rest of my brothers, some of the homes are occupied by more than one fey. However, Mya, Matt, and June are working with Ryan to establish a new settlement. Mya and Drav make the decisions for this settlement. Matt and June are making decisions for Tenacity. But it's still undecided who will help make decisions for Unity."

"Unity?"

"It's what Fallor said Emily would like to call the new settlement that's being built. She wants it to be a place where fey and humans can feel free to live together. Not in the same houses but in the same community."

"That sounds pretty nice. I know there are people in Tenacity who'd be willing to do that. A lot of them don't mind fey presence. They just feel like they're being pushed to pair up, which makes them uncomfortable."

Scath grunted as we continued down the street at a good clip. Moving around outside in the cooler temps wasn't so bad when a person was well-fed and warm. The morning walk felt nice and ended sooner than I would have liked.

Scath knocked on the door of a cute two-story home while I hung back behind him. When the door opened, I used one of my lenses to peer at the middle-aged man who'd answered.

"Good morning, Dad," Scath said. "This is Apryl. Her glasses were broken, and she needs them to be able to see. Can you help me make her a new pair?"

The man looked over at me with a smile already growing on his face.

"It's nice to meet you, Apryl. Come on in."

He waited until we were inside to introduce himself as Richard.

"I can't say I've ever tried making glasses before, but I love a challenge and a good distraction. Mom's in the kitchen.

Let me introduce you to her before we get lost in a new project."

He led the way to the kitchen and introduced me to Julie, a middle-aged woman with a kind smile and a welcoming hug.

"I've been hoping to meet you," she said. "What do you think of Tolerance so far?"

"I haven't really been out much but did meet Brooke and Solin. They seemed really nice. Hopefully I'll get to see more soon."

"She can't see without her glasses," Scath said. "Dad and I are going to try to make her new frames."

"I can't imagine how frustrating that must be for you," Julie said.

"Frustration has taken a backseat. Fear's mostly behind the wheel these days," I said.

Julie made a sympathetic sound.

"You two go on, then, and figure out a way to help her. She'll be fine with me. We'll whip up something to bring to Angel's at lunch and visit with her for a bit while we wait for you."

Scath set his hands on my shoulders and turned me toward him. I could see the concern on his face.

"Julie will keep you safe," he said.

"I'll be fine," I assured him. "You don't need to worry about me."

The guilt in his expression increased. "I will need your lenses."

It sucked surrendering them when I'd just gotten them back. But holding them like a dumb monocle for the rest of my life wasn't a practical option. Frames were. So I took the one out of my pocket and handed it over along with the other one I'd been using to see on the way here.

"Mom, without her lenses, she can trip on rugs and other

things she can't see. She shouldn't use knives or the stove. Please keep her safe."

With that demoralizing set of instructions, he left.

"Well that made me sound completely helpless and useless," I mumbled.

Julie laughed. "You're alive. That proves you're neither of those things. Come on, you can have a seat and tell me more about who you were before the earthquakes."

CHAPTER TWENTY-TWO

SCATH

"I'm glad you brought Apryl by," Dad said. "It'll distract Mom from worrying about Ryan while he's gone. Mom and Mya heard about Apryl and have been really curious. How did she come to live with you?"

I hesitated to tell Dad the truth, but like Emily and Mya, Mom and Dad wanted to help us find women willing to live with us.

"Matt and June's housing announcement is causing some females to be kicked out of their homes. Apryl came to me and asked if I had a spare room. Now that I know how poor her eyesight is, I don't believe she knew I was fey when she asked me. However, she knows now and says she would like to stay with me. She is frustrated that she cannot help me more. She believes she is deadweight and has no value to offer because she does not want to have babies. She thinks they will die because she can barely protect herself."

Dad was quiet for a moment as we walked toward Thallirin's where most of the woodworking tools were stored.

"I see. So fixing her glasses will help her realize she has value and make her more comfortable with living with you."

"Yes," I said, glad Dad understood.

"All right then. I guess we better figure out a way to make that happen. How many other women are losing their homes over there?"

"Fallor is watching. There are others, but he did not say how many."

"Is he working with Emily to approach them?"

"Probably. He knows they are less likely to say yes to a fey than they would be if she approached them."

Dad nodded. "He's smart. You're all smart and patient. That will pay off in the end."

I grunted, not wanting to disagree with him. My brothers and I were trying to be patient and not let our desperation show, but many of us were close to breaking. We were desperate to see our own females rounded with children.

When we reached Thallirin's house, Brenna was the one to open the door. Her hair was neatly pulled back in her usual ponytail, but her face was flushed, and her gaze a bit unfocused.

"We were hoping we could use the tools in the basement," Dad said, "but we can come back at another time."

"Nope. Now's perfect. I have to get to the meetup for feight club, or I'm going to be late." She glanced over her shoulder at Thallirin, who was standing shirtless in the hallway behind her. "I'll see you at lunch."

He nodded and watched her leave.

"Things going well?" Dad asked as he closed the door behind her.

"She refuses to listen to reason and continues to do what she wants," Thallirin said.

Dad chuckled and nodded. "Yep, that's women when you try to control them. Instead of telling her what to do, try asking her what she wants to do and then have a conversation about it where you voice your concerns. She might still do what she wants, but she'll be more willing to compromise so you feel better about her choice."

Thallirin acknowledged the advice and waved for us to follow him into the basement.

"Will Apryl be joining the other females at feight club today?" he asked as he led the way.

"No. Apryl cannot see well. We need to make her frames for her lenses first. Perhaps after, she will join the other females."

Thallirin stayed with us as I laid out the broken frame pieces and lenses. I explained my idea to recreate the frames from wood, and Dad and Thallirin helped refine the plan. We picked out the wood we thought would work best. Then Dad helped us cut some thin slices with the grain, which he thought would prove stronger.

While we started boring out the holes for the lenses, Thallirin left to see if Merdon might join us. Few of my brothers had his skill with wood.

We had to start the process over twice when drilling cracked the sides. But I had patience. I knew these things took time, especially when trying to do something new.

Merdon's arrival saved us from damaging another pair. He cautioned that they were taking too much off at once. Carving by hand was the best way to feel what the wood was willing to do.

So, each of us sat with a frame and began whittling in the basement.

"How's Hannah doing?" Dad asked. "Still having the nightmares?"

"Not every night," Merdon said. "And when she does, she no longer needs to go to the basement to remove those thoughts."

"Do you think she will change her mind about having children soon?" Thallirin asked.

Merdon shrugged. "She fears keeping an infant safe. She says losing one would break her completely."

"Apryl fears keeping an infant safe, too," I said. "The wall that protects us is sturdy, but if we want the females to eagerly bear our young, we need more." I looked at Dad. "What can we do?"

"That last breach shook people," Dad said. "The infected had been avoiding Tolerance, which we all thought meant they understood the danger here. However, the way they set up a decoy and found a way in showed that the infected were getting smarter. More daring. I don't know if higher, thicker walls will give the women the peace of mind they need. I think they need the infected dead. Maybe we need to take a lesson from the infected and start laying traps for them to reduce their numbers."

My brothers and I stopped whittling to stare at Dad. His suggestion made sense, yet, we knew how many infected were out there. Mya said millions. How could we kill that many?

"I know it sounds impossible," Dad said, "And it would be if it were just us humans. But I think if we work together, we could slowly reduce their numbers."

"How?" Thallirin asked.

"Well, think of that shipping center we went to. It had the food we needed and plenty of space for the infected to hide. They were smart enough to see that. We need to flip that around. Imagine if we found a space large enough to fit a lot of infected. A place we didn't care about and could bomb like we'd initially bombed the cities. If we could lure the infected there with light and maybe some sound recordings of humans, we could thin the herd."

Thallirin and Merdon looked thoughtful.

"It's not something Mya will like, especially after what just happened to Vorx," Dad said. "It puts whoever goes in an unhealthy amount of danger. However, trimming the numbers might help the women feel safer."

I exchanged a look with Thallirin and Merdon. Although they'd been forgiven for their parts in Olem's death, I could see their reluctance to agree to something that might endanger others.

"I will mention this idea to Drav," I said. "After watching Angel's belly grow round with child, many of us are eager to start our own families. If removing infected will encourage other females, it is something we should consider even if there is a risk."

Dad paused his carving to look at me. "Have any of you considered the risk of pregnancy? Mya's been pretty sick, which isn't uncommon. But the grey spots and the headaches might be more than pregnancy. Is it wise to rush into starting families when you don't know what carrying a hybrid baby will do to the mothers?"

My stomach churned at the thought of a baby harming Apryl, and when I glanced at Thallirin and Merdon, I saw similar reactions.

"Now, I'm not trying to cause any panic. I only want to make sure you're thinking things through. Drav and Mya didn't even know having a baby was possible. It wasn't planned, and now it is what it is. There's a lot we don't know and a lot we do. I think the women have a right to feel some reservations about getting pregnant."

I nodded thoughtfully, better understanding how Apryl might be feeling.

Yet, I also understood the importance of creating families with the humans. Each fey-human family would help create a bridge of acceptance that would encourage more fey-human families.

"What is your advice then, Dad?" Thallirin asked.

"Work on finding a way to decrease the infected population, but don't go to extremes just to rush having families. Be patient with your women if they aren't ready to start families, and pay attention to how the existing pregnancies progress. And above all, keep working together. You're excited to start your own families, but don't forget you were a family before coming here."

"You are wise. Thank you, Dad." I clapped him on the shoulder in a show of appreciation.

He coughed and winced. "Remember your strength, son."

I cringed and rubbed the spot I'd grabbed. "Sorry."

"Nothing's broken, and I'll live. Just don't forget around your pretty Apryl."

"Never," I swore.

He nodded. "How are your frames coming? Mine are looking like a beaver gnawed on them."

I glanced at his roughly shaped frames.

"Crafting with wood is like starting a family," Merdon said. "Both take time and patience."

"Well said," Dad said with a smile. "Let's see if we can get these ready for a test fit by lunch."

I set to work again, already imagining Apryl's delight when I presented her with functional glasses.

CHAPTER TWENTY-THREE

APRYL

"It's just about ready," Julie said, closing the oven door.

The scent of freshly baked bread was making my mouth water.

"I can't wait to try it," I said.

Julie joined me at the table and patted my hand. The last several hours had proven Julie to be the most welcoming and gracious woman I'd met since the fall of the world. I could see why one of her children was helping lead Tolerance, and the other was out building another version of it.

"You're a brave woman, Apryl. I'm not sure I'd be able to stomach what we did to that poor loaf of bread."

I chuckled, amused by her mock disgust and thrilled by her inclusion of me in the process of preparing lunch for Angel, a pregnant woman close to her due date.

"Pickles, ham, and cheese sound good to me," I said. "Hopefully, we adjusted everything enough so it doesn't come out underdone from the extra moisture."

"Even if it's a little underdone, she'll eat it. She's craving anything salty like crazy these days. I think it's the overabundance of sweets."

While I'd kneaded the dough and she'd chopped the pickles, she'd told me stories about the people living here. Little things that helped me feel more connected to the community I'd just moved into.

"Are you sure she's going to be up for company?" I asked. "I think I'd rather nap after a morning of exercise."

"Her exercise is limited to the cheering section these days. She told Mya it'll be her turn to motivate the rabble soon now that Mya's feeling better."

Although we'd heard rumors in Tenacity of Mya's pregnancy, I hadn't known how sick she'd been through the start of it. Her mom was concerned about the headaches she was still getting but was relieved they were less frequent. The grey spots that were expanding were another matter entirely.

"Do you think it's true?" I asked. "That sleeping with the fey is transferring the immunity?"

"Well, Cassie doesn't have any other explanation for how both Mya and Eden survived being bitten. Mya's pregnant. Eden isn't. What they have in common are those grey spots after unprotected sex with the fey. It's a logical conclusion and better than the one that some folks were saying."

I nodded, thinking of the men who'd hatefully claimed that sleeping with the fey was poisoning the women and how the infection spread in the first place.

The timer on the oven beeped, and Julie left the table to remove the bread.

"I'll leave this right here and get your jacket," she said. "You just sit tight."

She did more than return with my jacket. She returned with a fey to carry the bread so I could hold her arm while we made our way to Angel's house. Another fey, identifiable by the grey blur of his head, answered the door.

"Hi, Shax. Apryl and I made Angel some bread with pickles, ham, and cheese in it. Is she up for visitors?"

"Hell yes, she is," a woman called from somewhere in the house. "Bring that bread in here."

Julie chuckled as our fey escort passed the bread to Shax.

"Come in," he said, moving out of our way.

Julie didn't ditch me at the door but helped me out of my jacket and led me into the house.

"There's a rug coming up, and we're going to turn a corner here," she said, narrating the path. And I loved her even more for holding onto me because the rug was hard to see, and I did end up stumbling.

"Sorry," I said.

"That's like apologizing for the weather. Not your fault, and no need to worry. Put your hand out to feel for the chair, and have a seat."

"Holy shit, are you blind?" the woman asked.

"Not blind," Julie said, "Just visually impaired at the moment. Dad and Scath are trying to fix her glasses."

"Oh." The woman almost sounded disappointed, and I glanced her way.

"I didn't mean that in a rude way," she said. "It would have been cool if someone blind survived all of this, you know?"

"Who's to say someone didn't?" I asked. "When I was evacuated, I heard the soldiers talking about different evacuation sites. Some even up into Canada and on the other side of the Rockies. This is just one small corner of the world."

"Very true," she said as a chair scraped against the floor. "I'm Angel. It's nice to meet you, Apryl. So, how well can you see?"

"Not well. It's a miracle I'm alive, honestly."

While Julie served the bread, I told my story. Well, most of it. When it got to the part about mistaking Scath for a human, I hesitated.

"Shax, baby, would you mind hanging out with your brothers for a while so we can have some quiet girl time?"

He bent toward her and, from the sound of it, gave her a heated kiss before leaving without a word.

"Okay, we're fey-free," Angel said. "Now you can say whatever it was you didn't want to say without worrying about it being repeated."

Julie chuckled. "How do you know Shax was the issue and not us?"

"Pfft," Angel said. "She just moved here. It's obviously fey related."

I smiled slightly, enjoying Angel's blunt yet easygoing personality.

"It is fey-related. I made a huge mistake the day I met Scath. Several actually. Like I said, I kept my head down so I wouldn't call attention to the fact I couldn't see. Because of that, I had no way of knowing I was talking to a fey and not a human when the guy asked if I was looking for a place to stay. And then, when I returned to the same spot an hour later with my things, I had no way of knowing that the guy standing there wasn't the same guy, and he wasn't acting standoffish because he was hedging for a little physical payment for the room."

"No..." Angel breathed.

"Yep. I kissed Fallor. Twice actually. Once on the chin because I misjudged his height and again to correct the oversight. And I still didn't know I was dealing with a fey. That epiphany came after the kissing."

Angel groaned on my behalf while Julie patted my hand.

"Worse mistakes have been made," Julie said. "At least, you didn't try shooting him."

"Someone tried shooting one of them?" I asked.

"Eden," Angel said. "And Ghua forgave her in an instant."

"Yeah, well, Scath's going to need more time. I think he feels betrayed. He keeps telling me he needs to be sure that I'm not trying to kiss him out of some need to repay him for the food and a place to stay."

A beat of silence followed that.

"Do you have feelings for Scath?" Angel asked.

"If you're asking if I'm madly in love with him? No. It's too soon for that. But do I like him? Yes. He's pretty amazing. I never feel useless around him. He always finds ways for me to contribute to whatever we're doing. And he's kind and just... hot. That man has a body I want to bite. Is it shitty of me to say that?"

Angel laughed while Julie made a small sound of amusement.

"No, I don't think that's shitty at all," Angel said. "Physical attraction is a good thing. So is liking him. I wasn't in love with Shax right away. In fact, he was infatuated with another girl when I met him."

I sighed. "That's my biggest fear. That I'll lose my chance with Scath if another girl looks his way."

"First, I don't think that will happen," Angel said. "It's not typical for them to fall out of infatuation. Shax's case was unique. And second, if you're serious about wanting to move things along physically, just let him catch you masturbating. Worked like a charm for me."

I wasn't a prude by any stretch of the imagination, but I relieved I couldn't see Julie's expression after that.

"I heard it takes very little persuading for a fey to join in on any type of sexual activity," Julie said, surprising me.

"Well," I said, finding my voice, "I purposely fell over in

front of Scath, sans underwear, and he did nothing. Which is why I'm a little worried he's going to change his mind."

"Nah, you just need to nudge him over the edge. If he has one of those vibrating toothbrushes, masturbate with that. One taste of the fun zone and he'll be on you before you can squeal."

My mouth dropped open at her suggestion, and Julie chuckled and patted my hand.

"You remind me of Mya," she said. "She's open in so many ways, but she continues to try to stifle the fey's natural curiosity regarding females and sex. The fey are as fascinated as they are obsessed by both. So, Angel's idea isn't bad if you're brave enough to try it."

She nudged my plate, and the irony wasn't lost on me.

Not everyone was brave enough to try everything, but I was braver than most.

CHAPTER TWENTY-FOUR

SCATH

THE LENS AUDIBLY CLICKED INTO THE FRAMES, AND I TURNED THE piece in my hands, inspecting the wood for cracks. The sight of the unmarred surface filled me with pride but also impatience.

"This one worked," I said, already reaching for the other lens.

"Let it rest and adjust before adding the second one," Merdon said as he continued to whittle away at his frame.

His indifference to my accomplishment didn't upset me. After hours of trials, broken frames, and endless carving, we all knew a single lens fitting didn't mean success, which is why my brothers didn't stop their work. Their frames would be next if this one cracked like the many before it.

I glanced from the pile of thinly sliced wood Dad had been working on to the fading light coming from the basement's small window. The need to check on Apryl crawled under my skin. It didn't matter that Dad had checked on Mom and Apryl around mid-day or that he'd left again only minutes ago to do the same. I wanted to see Apryl for myself. I wanted to give her glasses that worked and watch the joy on her face as she put them on.

Instead, I still had nothing to show for my efforts except a growing frustration and a need to see her.

"How can you stand being away from your females for so long?" I asked, focusing on the frames in my hand. "How do you know they're safe?"

Merdon chuckled, a dry, dead sound. "We don't. We sit here and worry as much as you do."

"If you worry about them, why are you here? Why do you not go to them?"

"Human females do not like it when their males hover, which means to stand too close while worrying that they will hurt themselves," Thallirin said. "They prefer that we worry at a distance."

"Out of sight is better," Merdon said.

"You would prefer not to see them?" I shook my head. "I would prefer if Apryl never left my sight."

Merdon stopped carving and looked up at me. "The females call time away from their males 'me-time.' And you will learn the wisdom of granting your female freedom from your presence when you discover how eagerly she greets you afterward."

He had my attention. "How eagerly?"

Merdon smiled, something I hadn't seen in many lifetimes.

"Hannah used her mouth on me and refused to stop until I released. Then she begged me to mount her from behind." Merdon's expression grew distant, and he shook his head. "I released four times before I had the will to stop."

I shifted in my seat at the image he was painting. Only, in my mind, I saw Apryl on her knees, her rounded backside exposed to my view.

The door upstairs opened, distracting me from my thoughts. I turned my attention to Dad as he came down the stairs with a stack of wrapped plates.

"Good news from home," he said. "Ryan's back. He's found a location, and Shelby stopped by to say she found one too. Looks like we will have our third settlement."

It was good news, but my mind was filled with worry for Apryl. "Is Apryl okay, or is she ready to go home?"

Dad chuckled as he handed out the plates. "She's fine. She and Mom went to Mya's to check in on her. They'll head back to our house after."

Remembering Apryl's comments about keeping to herself before coming here and missing contact, I realized she probably *was* enjoying her time with Mom. Relieved she was doing well, I accepted the plate from Dad.

"Thank you."

"Anytime." He looked at Merdon and Thallirin. "I asked where your wives were too. Hannah's with Emily at Mary's, and Brenna is having dinner with Uan and Nancy. Now, let's eat up and get back to work so we're home before they miss us."

I set the frames aside and ate Mom's famous meat stew. When I finished, I returned to inspecting the frames for any stress cracks.

"Taking off a little more from the inner edge worked," I said.

Merdon grunted, and I started fitting the next lens. It fought the frame, and I paused to clear a little more material away before trying again. The lens snapped into place with another audible click.

I carefully turned the frames in my hands. Not a single fracture appeared.

Smiling, I handed it off to Merdon.

He inspected it just as closely and nodded.

"These will work. Now we need to attach the earpieces without creating cracks."

Well after dark, we left Thallirin's house. Merdon and Thallirin jogged off to reunite with their females while I remained beside Dad. The day had progressed better than I'd hoped. I had a working pair of glasses in my pocket and several more frames in various phases in the basement, which I planned to continue working on since the raw wood frames would likely crack with use over time.

"Adding a finish might change how the wood reacts when adding the lens. Maybe we should try different types of wood, too," Dad said, keeping his very human pace steady. "Pine is softer than oak, for example. It might crack less easily if there's more give."

Dad knew a little about finishing wood and said there were many ways. Oils. Lacquers. Paints. We had many options in the basement but didn't know which would work best. However, he was certain that frames with a finish would last longer...if they didn't crack when we tried adding the lenses.

The likelihood of that happening didn't bother me. Creating from nothing took time, patience, and the ability to learn from each attempt. But mostly patience. And I had plenty of that when it came to making glasses but very little when it came to seeing Apryl again.

"Drav mentioned trees in your caves that were more pliable for making bows. Maybe we should try some of that," Dad said.

The comment interrupted my thoughts of Apryl.

Since coming to the surface, I'd often thought of the caves and the brothers we'd left behind. However, I'd never considered the resources there we could use. Such as the plants we grew for medicine or food.

"I will mention that to Drav as well," I said, uncertain he would like the idea.

We all still felt the aftermath of my brothers' last return to the caves, and I doubted Drav would risk more lives for the sake of plants.

Thoughts of risk and my brothers evaporated when Mom and Dad's house came into view. The windows were lit, and the curtains were open so I could see Apryl sitting at the table in the kitchen. A sense of contentment and belonging filled me, and my step quickened.

Dad chuckled. "Drav does the same thing every time he sees Mya."

"Do you do the same when you see Mom?" I asked, slowing again.

"Sometimes. When I come back from a supply run, mostly. This world likes to remind us how precious life is and how we shouldn't waste even a moment of the time we have with the people we love."

I nodded slowly as his words settled in my mind. They were similar in sentiment to Apryl's thoughts of how uncertain her future was.

My fingers closed around the glasses, and I hoped again they would be enough to help her feel safer and more secure with her place in this world. And at my side.

Dad opened the door and called out, "We're home."

"About time," Mom called.

Rather than wait with Dad as he removed his jacket and shoes, I hurried forward and made my way to the kitchen.

Apryl looked up at me as I entered.

"Scath?" she said.

"Yes. Did you have a good day?" I asked as I bent to press my cheek to the top of her head. The scent of her hair filled my lungs and soothed me.

"I did. We went to Angel's house and visited for a while. Julie walked me around town again, showing me where everything is. She helped me shop for some more essentials at the storage house too. Then we visited Mya and Drav and heard about the new settlement. It's going to have a pond with fish in it."

Her hand settled on my arm. It wasn't quite a pat or a stroke, but something in between that made me want more. I rubbed my cheek against her hair again and turned my head to brush my lips against the soft strands before straightening away.

"Did you eat dinner?" I asked. "Are you hungry?"

"Yes, I ate. No, I'm not hungry. I'm impatient to hear how your day went. Are my lenses okay? Did you figure out a way to make new frames?"

Grinning, I withdrew the glasses from my pocket and put them into her hand.

"We made new frames. They are not as pretty or colorful as the frames you had and are more fragile, so you will need to take care. But we think they will work."

She ran her fingers over the earpieces and eased them open.

"If these break, do not worry. I will keep working on more frames until we find a pair that is durable."

She smiled slightly and lifted the frames to her face.

The moment they settled into place, her gaze shifted around the room, and her eyes began to water.

"I never thought I'd be able to see again," she said.

Then she lifted her gaze to me. She stared without saying anything, although her lips parted. Worry filled me, and I shifted uncomfortably, waiting for revulsion to twist her features.

CHAPTER TWENTY-FIVE

APRYL

THE GLIMPSE I'D GOTTEN OF SCATH THROUGH ONE LENS HADN'T done him justice. The man standing before me wasn't simply handsome; he was strike-me-dumb-with-a-stick hot. Abs for days. Pecs that could deflect a thrown quarter, thickly muscled thighs, and arms...oh, his arms. I wanted to pet them. All of him, actually, from head to toe.

But it was the expression on his face that did me in. He wasn't projecting the typical indifferent-player vibe most hot guys usually had. Instead, I saw his uncertainty, and it made me ache for him in a completely different way.

The fey hadn't been treated well by humans in general. They'd been shot at, spit at, and scorned. And, based on how he was looking at me, he was expecting me to whip out a side piece.

I was on my feet before I knew what I was doing and threw my arms around his waist. He rocked a little at the impact but immediately hugged me in return.

"Thank you," I said. "You have no idea how much having glasses means to me."

I tipped my head back and really looked at him. His eyes were amber-yellow, surrounded by a lighter green. And they had vertical slits, which were presently very narrow as he stared back at me. Unusual eyes but captivating with his long thick lashes. Laugh lines bracketed his wide mouth, adding to his appeal.

My gaze lingered on his mouth. I really wanted to try kissing him again now that I could see where I was aiming and knew who I was kissing. But I was very aware of our audience.

"Are you ready to go home?" I asked.

Surprise flickered in his gaze.

"You want to go home? With me?"

I barely swallowed my laugh at his disbelief.

"I do, Scath. I really, really do."

Releasing my hold from around his waist, I threaded my fingers through his. He led me toward the door as Richard and Julie followed.

"Thank you for coming by today," Julie said, pulling my attention from Scath. "It was nice having some company."

The middle-aged woman with hints of grey in her hair looked exactly like I'd imagined her.

"Same," I said. "I missed talking to people."

"Well, that phase of your life is done now," she said as Scath helped me into my jacket. "People here aren't like the folks in Tenacity. We aren't worried about limitations of the body, only those of the mind."

"Will we see you two tomorrow?" Richard asked.

I looked up at Scath, and he nodded. "I want to keep working on the frames, just in case these break."

"Sounds good. We'll see you in the morning then." Richard opened the door, and we waved our goodbyes as we left.

My breath clouded with my exhale, and I marveled at the

sight. At all of it, actually. The snow-dusted and well-tracked street. The lit-up homes. They weren't clear, but they were more than vague blurs of colors. And I could see the fuzzy shape of a fey—humans were smaller—crossing the street ahead of us.

"I missed you today, but these were well worth the time apart. I love my glasses," I said so Scath would know how much his effort meant to me. "I love being able to see. Especially you."

He watched me when I glanced at him and blinked a little like an owl when I took hold of his hand and smiled at him.

Deciding to be direct, I asked, "Has anyone told you how handsome you are?"

He blinked again.

"Since I'm not a mind reader, you're going to have to tell me if that blink is because no one has said it before or if it's because you don't believe me."

"Both?" he said, sounding uncertain.

"From the start, I knew you were nice, and I liked you for that. But I'm glad I didn't have my glasses until now. If I'd seen how good-looking you are, I probably wouldn't have agreed to live with you. Although, if I'd had my glasses, I wouldn't have messed up who to give my kisses to, and you'd believe me now."

"I don't understand," he said. "Why wouldn't you have agreed to live with me if you thought I was handsome?"

"Handsome guys tend not to want serious relationships until they've played the field a bit."

He frowned, his fingers smoothing over mine. "I don't understand what playing in a field has to do with a relationship."

"Ah...uh, what I meant is that really attractive men tend to have sex with a lot of random women rather than committing to just one woman."

He grunted. Twice.

"Are you all right?" I asked.

"You think I'm handsome."

"Yep, I do. Do you believe me?"

"Yes, but…"

"But?" I prompted after a few beats of silence.

"You wanted to trade sex for food and a home because you thought I would find another female I liked better. Now you think I will find another female because you think I'm handsome." He sighed. "How do I prove to you that I do not wish to find another female?"

"Well, you could start by having sex with me."

He snorted, a slight smile tugging at his lips.

"Sex only proves that you are willing to share your body, not that I have won your heart."

He stopped walking and cupped the back of my head, sending tingles of awareness shooting through my limbs.

"I am not hesitating to take what you're offering because I'm waiting for another female. I want your heart before I claim your body, Apryl."

I forgot how to breathe for a second, and when I did, it was a shuddering exhale.

"Wow. Love then. You want me to love you."

"Yes."

He released me and took my hand again. We walked the rest of the way to the house in silence. Mostly because I couldn't form a full thought.

Love.

I was with a guy who wanted love.

Wooing.

It would have been laughable if it wasn't so damn intimidating.

I didn't know how to woo. Hell, I'd already proven that I couldn't seduce him. Wooing was even harder.

He opened the door for me, and I walked in on autopilot before whirling to face him.

"I can't do it," I said.

He reached out and unzipped my jacket, his expression calm and focused on his task.

"You find me handsome and kind. I think you can."

I brushed a hand over my face, almost knocking off my glasses. He caught them and straightened them on my nose before easing the sleeves from my arms, avoiding eye contact.

"I've been trying to get you to sleep with me since I got here. You've seen me laid bare in embarrassing ways I'd rather not remember," I said with a wince. "My seduction skills are obviously non-existent. Falling for you would be easy for me, but I have no idea how to help you fall in love with me."

He stopped what he was doing and met my gaze.

"Fall in love with you?" he echoed.

The disbelief in his tone hurt more than I would have guessed possible.

"Ow. Okay. I get it. I've got my share of flaws, but I'm the kind of girl who wants to know she's the only woman in a guy's life. So this love thing will need to go both ways. If you want me to love you, you need to love me back. And if you don't think you can, let me know now."

His big hand captured the back of my head, and he pressed his forehead to mine.

"My heart is already yours, Apryl. It was yours the moment I saw you standing in line for food. I knew then that I wanted to be the male who would win your gaze and heart.

And now I have your gaze. I just need your heart. Fall for me, and I will catch you. I promise you are safe with me."

My heart was beating hard in my chest as my brain caught up to what was going on. Scath was telling me he loved me? It stunned me enough that I set a hand on his chest to steady myself.

I'd heard the fey fell hard and fast but didn't think it would be like this. Or with me. I thought I'd need to sleep my way into someone's heart. Actually, with what I was feeling under my palm, I was a little disappointed that it wasn't still on the table.

"You want my heart," I repeated before pulling back enough to focus on him. "I think a large piece of it is already yours."

"Good," he said, brushing his fingers over my cheek in the way I loved. "Are you tired, or would you like to watch a movie?"

"What would you like to do?" I asked.

"I would like to sit next to you on the couch and feel you right here," he said, resting his hand over his chest where I tended to rest my head.

"Then that's what I want to do."

He grunted and led me to the couch, asking me to sit while he picked out the movie. The second he settled next to me, I snuggled close so I was right where he wanted me.

I couldn't even focus on the movie as I struggled with the idea of what he wanted. It wasn't like I could just decide to give him my heart. That happened with time and a thousand little moments together. While everything he'd done so far had already won me over a good deal, I didn't see how I could give him everything he wanted when he was still holding himself back.

Sure, he touched my cheek and did that thing where he

grabbed the back of my head, which I liked. A lot. But it wasn't enough to really show that we had the chemistry I always looked for in a relationship. I needed more. I needed to know just how much he was attracted to me.

Lifting my head, I looked at his profile. The strong jaw. His perfect lips. That crazy, pointed ear.

"Scath, I want a kiss."

CHAPTER TWENTY-SIX

SCATH

ALL THE BLOOD IN MY BODY RUSHED TO MY COCK, AND I SHIFTED in my seat as I glanced at her. She mentioned kissing a lot. I knew kissing Fallor was a mistake she regretted, and she said that when she tried kissing me next, it would be because she was attracted to me. But she hadn't tried. Instead, she had asked for my touches and kisses. Touches, I could give without losing control. Kisses? I didn't think I could do that. I wanted her too much.

"Why?" I asked, stalling.

"Why?" she echoed, sounding a bit upset. "How can you say your heart belongs to me when you don't even want to kiss me?"

"I do want to kiss you."

"Then prove it." She pulled away from me, shifting her position to kneel beside me. When she leaned in, her breasts rubbed against my arm. My cock ached to the point of pain, and I winced.

She made a disgusted sound and started to get up off the couch.

"This is ridiculous," she muttered.

I hooked an arm around her waist to prevent her escape. She squealed and the back of her hand connected with the side of my face as I pulled her back down beside me.

"I can find food and cut wood and make frames for your lenses so you can see. I can kill infected and hunt the hellhounds without hesitation. But seeing your anger sends spears of fear through me. You are the only female who thinks I'm handsome and wants my touches and kisses. I don't know why, but I do know I would do anything not to lose you. Please don't leave."

She looked up at me, anger still in her gaze.

"Then kiss me, Scath."

The need to bury my fingers in her hair and take her mouth the way I wanted crawled through me. Instead of doing what I desired, I leaned forward and brushed my lips against her soft cheek.

She snorted.

"Seriously? You call that a kiss?"

"James kisses Mary like that. They love each other and have been married many years."

She blew out a breath and got back to her knees.

"I keep forgetting how new relationships are to you. Yes, that's a loving kiss, but it's not the kind of kiss I want from you right now. I want one that shows me how much you want me."

If I kissed her like that, I would break and take what she offered and hate myself for it. I wanted her heart, not her gratitude. Gratitude never lasted long, and I wanted her forever.

I knew I'd hesitated too long when she made an exasperated sound. Before I could guess her intent, she threw her leg over mine to straddle me. My hands caught her hips before she could settle her weight on my cock.

"It's just a kiss, Scath, not sex," she said, threading her

fingers through my hair. She brushed my ear, sending a shock of primal need straight to my cock. My grip on her tightened, locking her in place so she couldn't leave or press her sweet heat where I craved it.

"Well?" she said, leaning in. "Are you going to kiss me or not?"

I closed the distance between us and took her mouth. Her soft lips welcomed me, parting so I could taste her the way I'd been dreaming of. Her tongue danced with mine, teasing, tempting, demanding more. My fingers dug into her soft curves as I fought the need to settle her pussy over my hard length. The desperation to feel her there, to find my way home, consumed me. I shook with it as I devoured her mouth.

Just before the thin thread of my control could snap, I broke the kiss and set her beside me. She was blinking rapidly when I stood and strode away. I didn't know if I'd kissed her like she'd wanted and didn't stop to ask; I was two seconds from releasing in my pants.

As soon as I closed the bathroom door, I tore at my pants and clasped myself with a hiss.

I wanted Apryl. I wanted her so badly that I was no longer sure I would be able to hold out for her heart. The taste of her sweet lips still lingered on my tongue and made me wonder what other hidden coves I could be exploring with my tongue. Fisting my length, I found my release while imagining what sounds Apryl would make for me.

When I returned to the living room, Apryl was in the same spot I'd left her. She jerked her hand away from her mouth when she heard my approach and looked up at me.

"You ran again," she said.

"To the bathroom."

She stared at me for a long moment, saying nothing, then smiled slightly.

"Okay. I think I'm ready to go to bed."

I nodded, relieved I'd released when I had, or I wouldn't have been able to resist her breasts pressed against my side for very long.

Holding out my hand, I helped her stand. She leaned in, wrapping her arms around me and pressing her face to my torso.

"You're sleeping next to me tonight, right?" she asked.

"Yes."

"Good." Her hands smoothed down my back, making me wish I wasn't wearing a shirt. When she pulled back, I almost grabbed her again. But I didn't have to. She took my hand and led me to the bedroom.

I was so focused on the feel of her hand in mine that I didn't notice she'd stopped until she removed her glasses.

"Could you hold onto these for a second?" she asked.

"Yes."

As soon as her hands were free, she pulled off her shirt, exposing her bare breasts. I stared, and my mouth watered as I imagined burying my face between them to taste her skin. The nipples pebbled slightly, and I decided I would taste them too.

She reached down and unbuttoned her pants. Any relief I'd felt from my time in the bathroom evaporated as she slowly shimmied out of her jeans.

I couldn't decide what was more mesmerizing, the gentle sway of her breasts as she moved or each newly exposed inch of flesh.

She kicked her jeans free and, standing in nothing but her thong, plucked her glasses from my loose hold to place them back on her face.

"Thanks," she said. "Angel mentioned that the fey were learning to give massages. Would you be willing to rub my back? I think I was bent over funny when I was helping with lunch and strained something."

She turned away from me and crawled onto the bed on her hands and knees. My cock stirred at the sight of her rounded backside, and when she glanced back at me with a question in her eyes, I realized I still hadn't answered.

"Yes," I said roughly. "Where do you hurt?"

"Here," she said, touching her shoulders before lying flat on her stomach.

I moved to the side of the bed and sat beside her, my hands already smoothing over her skin.

"Mmm. That feels nice. Could you go harder? I like it deep."

I swallowed back a groan and used more pressure. The pleasure sounds she made were almost my undoing. Ignoring the steady throb in my pants, I continued to knead her sore muscles, drifting down her shoulders to her lower back. Angel told us to always stop there, but I itched to palm the fleshy curves of her ass.

"That's amazing, Scath. Thank you. Do you mind if I turn over so you can do my front now?"

My mind went blank as she rolled over. I stared at her breasts, remembering the stories I'd heard about how some of the females liked breast massages when they were sore. My palms itched to touch her there, and before I could stop myself, I did. She welcomed me with a soft sigh as I gently molded her flesh.

"Yes. Just like that," she murmured, her breathing coming faster. "That feels so good."

The ends of my ears grew hot, and my hands started to shake.

I abruptly stood.

"Don't go to the bathroom," she said, reaching for me.

"I'm not. I'm…I'll be right back." I hurried from the room. Her muttered curse followed me down the hall.

I was running again. I knew it. But I didn't know what else to do. If I'd remained there, fondling her beautiful breasts for another moment, I would have given in to my need to sink into her body.

And I couldn't do that. Apryl was in my blood, and I meant to have all of her.

CHAPTER TWENTY-SEVEN

APRYL

GROANING, I FELL BACK ONTO THE MATTRESS.

When we'd been on the couch and he'd winced after I'd asked for a kiss, I'd thought the worst. That he had zero interest in me as a woman. I couldn't have been more wrong. The kiss we'd shared out on the couch had told me everything I needed to know.

Scath wanted me. Badly. And he was only holding back because he doubted me. Us.

There absolutely was an us now. That kiss had erased any remaining reservation I had.

Scath was adorable. A keeper. He was kind, considerate, compassionate, and one hell of a kisser. I'd barely remembered my name by the time he'd finished with me. I'd been so sure I could help him past his reservations with a little persuasion of the smexy variety. Obviously, that hadn't worked. But at least I now understood why he kept running off to the bathroom. That raging boner he'd been sporting had been impossible to miss, thanks to my glasses.

Now, I just needed to figure out what to do about it. Should I follow him? Give him space? Talk to him about it?

Communication seemed to be our biggest problem. Either we weren't saying enough, or we didn't believe what the other person was saying. What kind of relationship would that make? Based on the last few days, a confusing and stressful one. And not one I wanted long-term.

Okay, then. Talking it was. However, we needed to level up our efforts in that department.

I looked down at myself, shrugged at my lack of clothing, then went to look for him.

Scath was pacing back and forth in the living room. And whatever thoughts were running through his head had him so distracted that he didn't even hear my approach. I leaned against the wall and just watched him. He ran his fingers through his hair then shook his head like he was having some kind of argument with himself.

"When you told me how much you didn't want me to leave, I thought it was kind of funny since you're the one always leaving."

At the sound of my voice, he paused his pacing and looked at me. The bulge in the front of his pants jumped, and he turned away, resuming his pacing.

"I had a lot of doubt before that kiss," I continued. "You were telling me that you wanted me, but you weren't acting like a guy who wanted a woman. Our actions and our words need to mesh, you know? So, here's what I propose. Complete, brutal honesty. Tell me what you want from me right now, and I'll do the same. And if what we want from each other isn't the same thing, then we'll talk about it—openly—like the adults we are, with respect for one another's feelings. Sound like something we can manage?"

He exhaled heavily. "I want you to put a shirt on. One I can't see through."

"Okay. What I'm hearing is that you want me to cover up. Can you tell me why?"

He glanced at me then studied the wall. "Angel said women don't like when we let our desperation show. It makes them want to leave." His gaze locked with mine. "But seeing you as you are now makes me very desperate, Apryl. I want to close the distance between us, hold you against that wall, and sink into your warmth. And if I did, I don't think I would be able to stop for days."

The heat that had begun to pool in my middle during his careful massage burst into something molten inside of me. I wanted the picture he was painting so fiercely that I had to swallow twice before I could speak.

"Yes, please."

"What?" His confused expression was so freaking adorable.

"Yes. I want what you just said—me against the wall for days. Facing you…facing the wall…bent over with my hands on the wall. All of it. I want it so much I'm having a hard time focusing on this conversation. And, for the record, desperation is only a turnoff if it's not mutual. And since our desperation for one another is mutual, seeing how much you want me only makes me want you more."

The long, hungry look he gave me before focusing on the wall spurred me on.

"But, I'll go put a shirt on. Will you come back to bed once I'm covered?"

"Yes," he said roughly.

Feeling both smug and a little disappointed, I returned to the bedroom and took one of his shirts from the closet. It hung to mid-thigh on me, which I hoped was enough coverage for him. Just to be safe, I got under the covers.

"Okay. It's safe," I called.

He looked so uncomfortable and uncertain when he entered the room that I patted the mattress beside me.

"No touching or kisses," I said. "I promise to keep my hands to myself for a while."

He grunted and joined me on the bed.

"I'm sorry for pushing, and I understand why you stopped. You still doubt why I'm here. But I want you to know I don't doubt you anymore. That kiss was the proof I needed to know you truly want me. So, I'm here for however long it takes until you believe I'm not trying to use sex to pay you back for a nice bed and a belly full of food. When we have sex, I want you to know, without any doubt, that I'm with you because you've pushed all my buttons in the best way."

"Buttons?"

"Yeah. The things that I really like in a guy. A kind heart. Good looking. Sexy voice. And an insatiable hunger for me." I smiled at him. "Plus, you're attentive without being controlling and can cook. Those were buttons I didn't even know I had."

I made myself comfortable and set my glasses on the nightstand beside me.

"So, tell me about making the glasses and what you'll be doing tomorrow."

The conversation was a little stilted at first, but the more he talked, the more he relaxed. And I could tell by the animated way he spoke that he truly was interested in what he was doing. For me. It made it even harder to keep to my side of the bed and not snuggle up to him.

"Does that mean I need to give up my glasses for the day?" I asked, rolling toward him. He was back to being a greyish blur again.

"No," he said, brushing his fingers over my cheek in the

way I loved. "I already test-fit the frames. You can keep your glass until the finishes are dry."

I was quiet for a second, debating how I wanted to spend my time while he was gone. Julie was nice and very welcoming, but I didn't think it was necessary to impose on her when I could see. Staying home was always an option, but without Scath here, it would get a little boring.

Angel had talked about feight club, where a bunch of the women got together to work out. It wasn't exercise as much as it was training to fight off an infected. I wasn't the fighting type. I was more of the run-and-hide variety. Before the earthquakes, I'd never been into spectator sports, but Angel made it sound kind of fun to watch.

"What do you think of me going to that feight club thing some of the women do? I wouldn't participate. I don't want to break my glasses. I'd just watch."

"I think you will enjoy it," he said slowly.

"What aren't you saying?" I asked.

He pulled me to his chest and wrapped his arms around me.

"You're mine," he said roughly, burying his head in my hair.

I grinned. "If you're worried some other fey is going to catch my eye, don't be. I've already kissed another fey, and Fallor did nothing for me. You, on the other hand, lit me up from the inside with your kiss. You're the only one I want."

He grunted and continued to hold me, which was just fine. I loved snuggles, especially when my face was pressed up to that wide expanse of muscled chest.

I fell asleep in his arms and woke up in them for the first time ever.

"Morning," I mumbled, rubbing my face against his skin.

Frowning, I pulled back a little to look at him.

"When did you lose the shirt?" I asked. "Not that I mind. Just curious."

"When I went to the bathroom."

I nodded slowly. "Are you going to the bathroom to stroke one off?"

He blinked at me.

"Masturbate," I clarified.

He remained quiet, so I twisted around to grope for my glasses. When they were sitting on my face, I saw a dark stain on his cheeks but an even darker one on his ears.

"Hey, I'm not judging. After that boob rub you gave me, I was close to taking care of business myself." I ran my fingers over his chest. "I kind of like that you want me so much you keep sneaking off."

He grunted, caught my hand, and brought my fingers to his mouth.

"Do you still want to go to feight club?" he asked.

"Yeah, I think so."

"We should get up then. I'll make you breakfast while you get ready. Dress warmly."

"Okay." I watched him get out of bed, staring at his shorts-clad ass as he left.

When he was gone, I stretched languidly and thought of the day ahead. I'd met Brooke, Angel, and Mya, all women close to my age, and Julie. They'd all been great. But Brooke and Angel had been so forthcoming with their information. I needed more of that. I wasn't sure what to do about Scath's understandable hesitancy. How did I undo the mistrust I'd created by kissing someone else in front of him?

After I dressed, I joined him in the kitchen for a quick reheated breakfast from the day before. Then we were out the door.

CHAPTER TWENTY-EIGHT

SCATH

Walking away from Apryl was just as difficult that day as it was the day before. But I couldn't delay speaking with Drav any longer. Not after what she told me last night. Apryl wanted me. Me. Not the house, not the food, but me. However, she did not want babies.

While watching Apryl sleep, I'd thought a lot about what our future would bring. I wanted children. But not without Apryl. And I understood her reasons for not wanting them immediately. The humans still had much to fear from the infected.

My brothers and I needed to end their fears, and Dad's suggestion was a good way to start.

Drav answered the door after a few moments. He looked more relaxed as he stepped back to let me in.

"Good morning. Is Mya awake?" I asked.

He shook his head. "She was up earlier but likes sleeping more now."

I was relieved she wouldn't be present for this conversation since I didn't think she would agree with Dad's ideas.

"My new female, Apryl, does not want pregnancy. She says

there are too many dangers. Too many ways for our children to die. Merdon and Thallirin say their females think the same way. What if this is why the females in Tenacity are reluctant to participate in all the things Emily planned? What if their fears are why more of our brothers do not have females of their own?"

Drav looked thoughtful.

"What you say makes sense. Mya kept running from me when she was afraid. She stopped running when we reached Ernisi."

"We need to stop only killing the infected that come close to the walls and hunt the infected like they hunt us. Set traps. Gather big groups of them. Dad suggested we use bombs. We have witnessed how those damage what the humans have built and can kill the infected just as easily with our hands."

"I like this idea. I will speak with Ryan to see if he has any ideas for trap locations."

"There is another thing we need to consider," I said. "We left our home and all that we've worked to create. So much of the human world has been destroyed. They struggle with food and medicine. We are collecting seeds for them to grow when the weather warms, but they will take time to mature. There are plants and medicines in the caves that the humans might find useful. If we are truly never returning to our old lives in the caves, should we bring some of the plants we know here?"

"You're suggesting we go back?" he asked.

"I am. We rarely fall ill. When we do, our medicines help us. What if those are the medicines that our children will need."

Drav sighed. "You are wise to think this way."

"Dad, Thallirin, and Merdon are wise. I am desperate enough for children of my own that I will speak ideas that might help me gain them even when I know such ideas might result in losing another one of our brothers."

Drav nodded gravely. "There is much to consider. Thank you for speaking to me. I see I must speak to Merdon and Thallirin as well."

"They have survived many lives alone and likely have knowledge that could prove useful if you can persuade them to share it," I said, walking to the door.

"Why would they not?"

"They fear being blamed for any resulting deaths and losing the family they've gained."

"I would never send them away from their females."

"It's not their females they fear losing. They love their females and would never leave them," I said. "It's us they fear losing again, Drav. Olem's death will forever influence their actions. I believe they no more meant to kill Olem than you meant to kill Phusty."

"Mya has said the same," Drav said. "I will speak with them."

I nodded and left, making my way back to the feight club. Apryl sat next to Angel, watching Brenna and Hannah wrestle on the ground. Angel was cheering while Apryl looked concerned.

When my shadow fell over Apryl, she glanced at me and popped to her feet.

"Scath. I didn't think you'd be back this soon."

"Aw, do you have to go?" Angel asked.

Apryl slipped her hand into mine. "'Fraid so. Thanks for inviting me, though. It was interesting seeing what you do."

Angel grinned a little. "Take it you won't be back tomorrow?"

"My nose is cold, my glasses are steaming up, and I'm terrified that Hannah's going to make me wrestle her next."

"I'll be good to you," Hannah yelled as she circled Brenna.

"Our ideas of good differ, but I appreciate your effort and know to start screaming your name if I ever need help."

Hannah flashed a grin at Apryl just before she sprang at Brenna. Apryl tugged my hand, leading me away as she called to Angel, "Let me know if you ever want a visitor. I'll hang out at your house anytime."

Angel waved goodbye to Apryl and focused on shouting her support to Brenna.

"Did you get too cold?" I asked.

"Cold and terrified," she said. "I was ready for the cold, but I wasn't ready to witness how viciously those women train. I thought I could watch it, but I can't. Brenna was one forearm block away from a collapsed trachea. At least, that's how it looked to me."

I wrapped my arm around her and pulled her close to my side.

"I'm sorry I took you there. I didn't intend to add to your fears."

"Don't worry about it. I'll forget what I witnessed. Eventually. Are you done working on the frames already?"

"No. I haven't yet started. I spoke with Drav first then came back to ensure you were warm enough."

"I'm glad you did," she said. "I was trying to think of a polite way to leave without hurting Angel's feelings."

I kissed the top of Apryl's head because she was such a good, caring female. But also to breathe in her scent. I'd missed her even though I hadn't been gone long.

"Since you did not wish to return home, do you wish to visit with Mom?" I asked.

"Sure. That sounds more my speed."

When I dropped her off at Mom and Dad's, Dad was waiting to walk to Thallirin's with me.

"You both take a break today and come home for lunch," Mom said as Dad kissed her cheek.

I glanced at Apryl. She smirked at me and tapped her cheek, inviting my kiss. If I were smart, I would kiss her there, where it was safe. But I didn't want safe. I wanted Apryl to feel my hunger for her so she would not forget how much I wanted her after I was gone.

She squeaked when I looped an arm around her waist and pulled her flush against me.

"The wall," she murmured. "The wall."

The image of her against the wall overrode my good intentions. Grabbing both her hands, I tugged them over her head and backed her into the wall. Her breath whooshed out of her, and she looked up at me with parted lips. It was all the invitation I needed. Ducking my head, I took what she offered and didn't stop until her lenses were fogged.

"I will return for lunch," I said, gently kissing her forehead before leaving with Dad.

"Well, the two of you seem to be getting on better," I heard Mom say as Dad closed the door.

Dad chuckled. "The glasses worked then?"

"She is happier with her glasses and likes looking at me." I couldn't stop the joy that spread at telling him that.

"I bet she does. Seemed to like kissing you too. Does that mean she's staying?" Dad asked.

"Yes. She wants to stay with me. I don't think she will be ready to have babies soon, though. She still has many fears. I did speak to Drav. He liked the idea of hunting the infected as they hunt us. He said he will speak to Ryan when he returns to see if Ryan has any ideas regarding where to set traps."

"I'm glad Drav is considering it," Dad said.

"I also spoke to him about the food and medicines we left behind," I said. "He may consider going back for those as well.

But I don't think any of that will change Apryl's fear of having a baby. Mya is pregnant. Eden has a thing in her arm to prevent pregnancy and Nancy takes pills. I think some of the other females are taking them too. What happens when we run out of pills?"

"Let's focus on today's problems and let the others wait for their day, okay? And there's always abstinence if you're really worried."

I cringed at the thought, and my testicles ached like Apryl hit them with her knee again.

"I can see that's not your favorite option." Dad patted my back. "Let's hope it's not a choice you ever have to make. Ready to get to work on those frames?"

CHAPTER TWENTY-NINE

APRYL

"So, what do you think I should do?" I asked Julie.

"Well, I understand your concern about becoming pregnant. A lot of the women here are worried about that. A few have managed to get their hands on birth control, but most of it's going to Nancy, who would be too high risk with our limited resources if she were to get pregnant. Her words, not mine. And to Brenna and Hannah, who aren't ready because of the emotional trauma they've endured. Jessie's trying to time things and uses condoms during her fertile window. So far, she seems to have been lucky doing that. Eden has an implant, I believe. Mya and Angel are both already pregnant. I'm not sure what everyone else is doing, honestly."

"So you think I should just let things be and be grateful we're not having sex?"

"I didn't say that."

I made a face at her. "You're not helping."

She laughed. "You need to do what feels right for you. If abstaining is what feels right for now, then do that. If you'd rather not wait to affirm your feelings for Scath, see if he'd be willing to go out and look for birth control for you. I've heard that Uan's been having luck in Warrensburg. It gets a little messy with the infected lingering there, but he stops at a lake to wash up before returning home."

I inwardly cringed at the idea of asking Scath to face infected just so I could avoid pregnancy. Yet, the idea of being pregnant still terrified me. Sure, I had glasses and could now see people who were within ten feet of me, but how safe was that? Could I outrun an infected if they were within ten feet? Doubtful.

Groaning, I set my head in my hands.

"The people here have embraced the 'one day at a time' approach to life since the quakes," Julie said. "Maybe that's what you should try doing too. But I do want you to know that if you do end up pregnant, you're not alone. We all watch after Mya and Angel. Every fey and human here. The children they carry are the future of this world, and I don't know a single person who wouldn't give their life to see a better future than what we're living now."

Her words helped calm my fears enough to help with lunch preparations. However, by the time Scath arrived with Richard, I still wasn't sure how I wanted to handle things between us.

And then Scath decided for me.

He walked right up to me, took my hands in his, and pinned them above my head. His hungry smile before he lowered his head set my heart racing as much as the intensity of his kiss. He set everything on fire with so much ease that I felt like I would combust if he didn't do more.

I wiggled my hands, trying to free them so I could touch him in return, but he didn't give me an inch as he rocked my world. Breathless and growing more desperate, I arched against him, hip to hip.

He broke away and looked down at me. "Did you miss me?"

I was breathing so hard I couldn't speak.

"Scath, son, you might want to give the poor girl a moment," Richard said, reminding us of their presence…in *their* house.

I flushed as I glanced at them both. "Sorry."

Julie grinned and shook her head. "We've been around the fey long enough to know what kind of greetings they like to give. If you're ready, we can sit down for some lunch."

I looked up at Scath and wiggled my hands, which he was still holding against the wall above my head.

"Time to let me go," I said.

He did but with an expression of disappointment.

I patted his chest. "You can do that again later. And yes, I missed you."

He grinned, and I realized then that there would be no holding out or worries about pregnancy when the time came. He'd simply pin me to the wall, and I'd forget every fear I had. But how would I feel afterward?

We ate lunch together, and I listened as Scath and Richard explained what they were doing to create the frames. Then Julie and Richard told us about Unity's progress and the changes that had been taking place in Tenacity the last few days.

"I'm glad the soup kitchen is still going," I said. "I know I can't have been the only one depending on it."

"You weren't," Julie said. "Matt and June know there are some people still looking for houses and have invited them to help out at Unity. They'd have to cohabitate with a fey or two for safety, but no one seems to mind it so far. Everyone's pitching in to get that wall built as quickly as possible."

"Has Emily found a lot of skilled people?" I asked. Julie

had already mentioned Emily's quest to find people with useful skills who could teach other people those skills.

"A few. Some people can knit or make bread. Mary knew how to make a sourdough starter. And when Richard, Ryan, and the fey put their minds to figuring out how to make something, they do pretty well. Just look at the wood stoves and solar. I just wish we had more doctors and veterinarians."

"More animals, in general, would be good," Richard said.

Julie reached out and patted his hand. He turned his and held hers in the way that couples did when they were together for a long time.

"Are you ready to go?" Scath asked, noticing that I'd finished eating.

"You don't need to go back to Thallirin's?" I asked.

"No. I am ready to go home with you."

All the tingles that had faded from that kiss stormed back with a vengeance.

"Okay," I said.

"I hope we see you tomorrow," Julie said. "Emily's hosting a knitting class, and I think someone is doing some cooking if you're up for it."

"Um, I'll let you know," I said, bringing my plate to the sink.

Scath and I helped wash the dishes before heading out. Earlier in the morning, I saw a few fey walking the streets. There were twice as many now. They nodded to us as we passed, and Scath pulled me a little closer to his side.

"So, what do you want to do for the rest of today?" I asked as we drew closer to the house.

"We can watch a movie," he said.

"Sounds good to me."

He opened the door for me, and I went in, already unzipping

my jacket. But my mind wasn't on what I was doing or the movie we were going to watch. It was on the new community and Emily's efforts to find people with skills and how, maybe, I was thinking all wrong. Maybe we weren't in the middle of an apocalypse. Maybe we were on the tail end of it. Maybe it was okay to think of rebuilding and a future that didn't involve dying.

I hung up my jacket and looked at Scath.

"When I'm with you, I forget all the reasons I'm afraid. I forget to *be* afraid. Back in Tenacity, I would have kept my head down on my walk home. My ears would have been straining for infected moans or panicked screams. I would have already been planning where to run and where to hide. But just now? There wasn't any of that. I was looking at everyone we passed and nodding back to them.

"You make me feel safe, Scath. And when you pull that 'pin her to the wall' move? I feel so loved and wanted. I want you to feel that, but I don't know how to give that to you. Tell me what to do to show you how much I care about you. Because I don't want to wait to be with you. Everyone's working so hard to embrace the possibility of a future, and I'm just here, standing still."

His hand cupped the back of my head, and he pressed his forehead to mine.

"You love me," he said.

"I think I do. I can't say I've ever been in love before to know. But I can say that I've never felt for anyone what I feel for you. I want to use you as my pillow every night until the day I die. I want to cook meals with you and laugh with you. And the idea of maybe having babies with you someday isn't as terrifying as it was because I know you and all the other people here will be with me, keeping me and whatever kids we have safe."

He lifted his head to brush a kiss against my brow. Then another one a little to the right of it.

"Does this mean you believe me?" I asked.

He took my hands and pinned them to the wall above my head.

"I believe you," he said.

Then he claimed my lips, and nothing else existed but Scath.

CHAPTER THIRTY

SCATH

My heart pounded in my chest as I claimed Apryl's lips. She was mine. Truly mine. She loved me. She wanted to live the rest of her life with me. My hunger for her intensified, and I released her hands to grasp her hips. Her fingers threaded through my hair, and she moaned as I lifted her.

Pinning her against the wall with my weight, I ground my aching cock against her, giving her what she'd said she wanted. Another small sound escaped her. Each one teased me and drove me to wring another from her and another until her legs wrapped around my waist and she moved in time with my slow thrusts.

She tore her mouth from mine, panting.

"Scath, please. I need you."

"Tell me what you want," I said, kissing my way down her throat. "Do you want these gone?" I pulled back enough to rub a hand over her jean-covered core. "Do you want me to sink into your pussy while I hold you against the wall, or do you want me to bury my tongue there first?"

"Yes," she panted, pulling on my hair. "All of it."

I chuckled and held her against me as I strode to the

bedroom, punctuating each step with a nip to her collarbone. The ragged sound of her breathing filled the air and fed my need. When we reached the bed, I placed her on the mattress and unbuttoned her pants.

"My mouth waters for a taste of you," I said as I worked. "I've thought of little else. Waking. Sleeping. My cock has ached with my need to taste you on my tongue."

"Yes," she panted. "More."

"More what?"

"Tell me what you've been thinking."

Her pants came free, exposing her thong. I hooked my fingers in the thin material and pulled.

"I've been dreaming of parting your beautiful—what happened to your pretty curls?"

The once thick thatch of beautifully curled down was nothing more than a mismatched patch of stubble and skin. I gently ran my fingers over her once lush folds in sorrow. They glistened wetly, though, distracting me from the travesty. As did the way her legs fell to the side, parting her wide.

"It'll grow back," she panted. "Tell me you still want a taste."

I licked my lips and nodded, suddenly too parched to speak. Instead of answering, I dipped my head and ran my tongue along the right side of her dripping slit. We groaned in unison as the lightly salted yet sweet flavor hit my tastebuds. It was better than my brothers had said. Thousands of times better.

Gently, I lapped the left side, hungry for the feast she would offer me. For a lifetime.

"Tell me you love me," I said before stroking my tongue over that little bump that made some females squeal.

"I love you, Scath," Apryl said with a sigh.

"And I love you, my Apryl," I said, dipping my tongue

into her core where the taste of her was concentrated. I lost myself in the pleasure of tasting her for several minutes, listening to her breathing increase until she shouted and her core pulsed against my tongue.

"Yes," I breathed between licks. "You are so pretty, my Apryl. So giving. Tell me I can continue."

"I need a minute," she panted.

I removed my mouth from her folds and kissed the inside of her thighs. Using my gentle bites to distract her, I eased a finger into her channel.

She made a contented sound, and I smiled, knowing she would welcome more attention once her pulse returned to normal. Setting a slow pace, I moved my finger in and out several times then added a second one.

"How can that feel so good this soon?" she mumbled.

"Your body is eager to welcome me." I placed a light kiss on that little bump in her folds, and she jumped. "Not yet, but soon." I soothed her with another kiss on her thigh.

When I added a third finger, her tight channel fought me.

"I think it's time for another taste."

"Wait, I think—ah!"

Her core clenched around my fingers as I caught that little nub between my lips and gently suckled. Then she opened for me, and my fingers moved in and out of her with ease.

I stroked her a few more times as I stripped off my pants. She only felt a moment of emptiness before I positioned my cock at her entrance and pressed into her. The tightness returned, and I knew from my brothers not to force myself inside but to work my length in inch by inch.

"Yes," I said. "That's my beautiful female."

I shook with my need for release but refused to give in to the urge until she clenched around my shaft. It was unlike anything I'd ever felt and better than I had imagined.

Her nails dug into my back, and her hips began to rise in time with mine, pulling me deeper.

"Yes," she panted. "Like that. But more."

I rotated my hips and finally sank all the way home. Pausing there, I waited, giving her time to fully accept me as I struggled for control. Her wet heat branded me. The need to move in the warm, welcoming depths that gripped me threatened to rob me of every thought.

She swore under her breath and wiggled under me.

"Too much?" I rasped.

"No. No. Just give me…" She wiggled again. "Scath, you need to move. I was so close."

Understanding what she meant, my control snapped. I braced one arm next to her head and reached under her ass to tilt her hips.

We both made relieved sounds when I started a new, frenzied rhythm.

"Yes," she panted. "Yes. Harder."

I didn't give her what she wanted. She would be sore as it was, and I knew one release wouldn't be enough. She tightened around me, crying out and milking my shaft until I joined her. Pulse after pulse, I emptied myself into her.

After the last one, I bent my head and kissed her tenderly.

"You are mine, Apryl. Today and every tomorrow after. Forever."

"Forever," she agreed weakly. "Especially with the moves you have. I'm never leaving."

"You liked it?"

"I loved it. I can't wait to do it again."

I gently moved in and out of her. "Then we won't wait."

Her eyes went wide as she looked up at me.

"I thought the rumors were an exaggeration."

"What rumors?" I asked, not pausing.

"The ones that said you never went soft and could have endless sex."

I chuckled. "Too much sex will hurt you. One more time, and then we'll rest," I promised.

She insisted on two more times before she closed her eyes and fell asleep. I held her in my arms and drifted off, feeling a contentment I'd never before had.

Apryl was mine.

Forever.

EPILOGUE

APRYL

I knocked on Angel's door and tried not to let any of my anxiety show. During the weeks I'd been here, I'd learned the fey saw everything and heard even more. And I didn't want to give any hints as to what was going on. At least, not yet.

Shax opened the door, impatience stamped on his face.

"Hey, Shax. Is Angel home?"

"She's not feeling well."

"Shax! Don't you dare," Angel yelled from inside. "I'm just fine."

He frowned but stepped aside to let me in.

"Everything okay?" I asked him as I took off my jacket.

"He's anxious," Angel said, waddling her way toward me. "Ninja has stopped kicking for cupcakes. He's still moving around. I can feel him. Shax is just freaking out, which is going to make me freak out. So Shax is going to go have a nice visit with whoever he wants, except Cassie, and let me have one hour of peace where I get to visit with Apryl. Right, Shax?"

Angel sounded so unlike herself that I glanced at Shax to see if he knew what to make of her.

He nodded, kissed her cheek, and fled.

Angel turned her slightly angry scowl at me and rubbed her side.

"I'm really glad you're here," she said softly. "I was trying to keep my cool around him, but it was cracking."

"Is everything okay?" I asked again.

"Yeah. Just nature running its course. Come on, let's sit down, and you can tell me what brought you by."

I followed her to the living room, noticing her slower gait and more pronounced waddle. When she turned to sit on the couch, I also saw how much bigger her belly looked under the Shax-sized t-shirt she wore.

"How much longer until the Ninja gets here?" I asked.

"That's all up to mother nature," she said as she settled into place, slowly rubbing her hands over her belly.

I hesitated to ask the question I really wanted to ask.

"Are you excited?" I asked after a moment.

"Honestly? I'm scared shitless. I'm afraid it's going to hurt. That something is going to go wrong. That I'm going to die trying to bring a baby into a world that is absolutely not baby-proofed."

I felt my nose start to tingle with tears and couldn't stop them from spilling over.

"Aw shit. You're pregnant, aren't you? And you came here looking for some support and encouragement," Angel said softly.

I nodded.

"I'm sorry. Today's not the best day for that. I'll probably have more positive things to say tomorrow."

Before I could ask why tomorrow, she winced, and a gush of liquid soaked the couch.

"Don't say anything," she said forcefully. "Not one word."

I nodded, understanding.

"I just need a minute to think." She waved me over and

held out her hand. I took it and let her squeeze it through a contraction. Probably not her first.

"I was scared," I said. "I wanted to talk to you because you always seemed so calm about being pregnant. I guess I wanted you to talk me down from a ledge. But Julie gave me the answer weeks ago. She said that if I got pregnant, I wouldn't be doing it alone. And she wasn't just talking about Scath. She said that every person here would give up their lives to keep a baby safe because our kids will be our future.

"That doesn't erase the fear of the delivery. But I guess it gives a meaningful purpose to everything we endure to help make that future possible."

"Okay, Yoda. You're here for the long haul, now," she said with a half-smile that turned to a grimace.

Once that contraction passed, she very quietly told me what to do.

I hurried to the door.

"I need the nearest fey to go get Cassie, Kerr, Julie, Shax, Solin, and Garrett. Angel's baby is coming."

Several of the nearby fey took off at a sprint. Others ran toward the house. I closed the door before they could ask questions, just like she'd said.

"Message delivered and fey running for your people," I said, hurrying back to her side.

She was breathing through another contraction, and I took her hand. When she finished, she looked at me.

"Tell me everything will be okay," she said.

"Everything *will* be okay," I said. "Women have been giving birth since the ice age, right? And we've gotten a whole lot smarter about how to do it safely."

She gave me a grateful smile as the door opened. Cassie hurried in as Kerr closed the door behind her.

The redhead, who I'd met once before, glanced at Angel,

who was squeezing my hand again, then handed me a watch.

"Tell me how long between this one and the next one, okay?"

"Okay."

"Looks like your water broke, Angel," Cassie said. "Did the contractions start before or after?"

The door opened again.

"Before," Angel answered. "They woke me up."

"Why didn't you tell me?" Shax asked.

"Because babies take time, and I didn't want you freaking out," she snapped.

He frowned, looking sad, and Cassie glanced at him.

"Remember how hormones can make the moods swing? This is like that. Try not to take it personally. I'd like your help setting up the bed, okay?"

They disappeared upstairs, and I marked the time as another contraction started.

The door opened again, and Julie entered with a man I'd never met.

"Hi, sweetheart," Julie said, hurrying into the living room. The guy stayed by the door.

"I'm here, Angel," he said. "Do you need anything? A pickle? Snack cake?"

Angel gave a strangled laugh. "A pep talk if you have one."

"There are at least fifty fey outside this house, all waiting to greet my niece or nephew. That's at least fifty willing diaper changers for you."

She laughed again, but I could see the fear in her eyes that she was trying to hide.

"We're all set," Cassie said, coming back down the stairs with Shax.

When he walked toward her, she released my hand, and I got out of the way.

Scath was always careful with me when he was picking me up and carrying me around, and having his way with me. But the way Shax handled Angel was something else entirely. Like she was a landmine, and one wrong move and she'd explode, which was probably right.

"Stop," she said. "I need to walk."

Cassie waved for him to put her down.

"She'll tell us what she needs," she said. "She's listening to her body, and we should do the same."

"Come on, sweetie," Julie said, taking her hand. "Think you can get up those stairs?"

Angel nodded and looked at Shax. "Behind me. Get ready to catch."

I wasn't sure she was talking about her or the baby she was carrying.

"How far apart are they?" Cassie asked me softly.

"A minute," I said.

She made a face and glanced at Julie, who nodded.

"Do you feel like pushing, Angel?" Julie asked.

"Someone down the stairs? Yes. This baby out? Not yet. Ninja can stay a little longer."

"We have nothing to worry about, Angel," I said as she made her way up the stairs. "We've got this."

She glanced back at me, nodded, and started moving a little faster.

The door opened again.

"They're upstairs, Solin," the guy by the door said. "Better hurry. Doesn't sound like the baby's going to wait for you."

The fey took the stairs two at a time before the guy came over and looked at the wet cushions.

"My name's Garrett. I'm Angel's adopted apocalypse brother. Any chance you're willing to help clean the couch?"

We worked together and listened to the sounds coming

from upstairs. My stomach churned with every grunting groan from Angel and each low murmur of words. Garrett paced. I sat on the dry cushion and tried to will everything into being okay.

When there was a sudden squeal, I sprang to my feet. Garrett beat me to the stairs.

"I need an update," he said.

"Angel is tired but doing fine," Julie called.

"And the baby?" he asked.

"It's a girl."

That was it. Nothing else.

He and I shared a look, and he returned to his pacing.

Unable to take the suspense, I went upstairs and peeked into the bedroom. The towels between Angel's legs were bloody, which freaked me out. Shax, too, by the looks of things. He was kneeling on the floor beside the bed, not looking between her legs at the still-connected baby but at Angel.

I didn't look at her. My eyes were locked on the baby.

The little girl flailed her arms and legs as she cried, which seemed normal enough. Her coloring wasn't, though. Her body was a patchwork of grey spots and pale skin.

"Why won't they let me hold her, Apryl," Angel asked. "What's wrong with her?"

I glanced at Cassie, who was examining every inch of the infant and listening to her heart, then met Angel's gaze.

"I don't think anything is wrong with her any more than anything is wrong with Mya or Eden," I said. "She has grey spots."

Angel held out her arms. "Give her to me."

Julie wiped a wet rag over Angel's forehead, smoothing back her hair as Cassie removed her stethoscope and picked up the baby.

She settled her on Angel's stomach, and the baby immediately turned her face toward Angel's skin.

A hand settled on my shoulder, and I glanced back to see Scath there. His gaze held mine for a long moment before he looked at the scene in the bedroom.

"She seems fine," Cassie said. "Her lungs sound clear, and her pulse is strong, which is good. We'll give you both a moment, and then Julie can wash her while we take care of the rest."

"There's more?" Shax asked.

"The afterbirth," Cassie said.

Scath tugged me away from the room and down the stairs.

Garrett watched us. "Are they both okay?"

"Yeah," I said. "They seem fine. I mean, Angel's going to need some serious recovery time, but they're good."

He nodded and sat on the clean cushion. "Might not want to go outside yet," he said. "You'll be bombarded with questions. I think Shax wanted to make the announcement."

Scath picked me up and sat in a chair with me in his lap.

"I understand why females fear having babies," he said, holding me close. "We don't need to have any."

I made a choked sound. "It's a little late for that, Scath. I'm pregnant. I just took the test this morning."

"Are you afraid?" he asked softly.

I leaned into his hold, soaking up his warmth. "A little. But I have nine months of pampering to help me forget about it."

There were footsteps on the stairs, and we looked up at Shax, who was carrying a wrapped bundle.

"Come look, Garrett," he said.

Garrett went to his niece and frowned.

"Mya showed me her spots," I said. "One is the size of a half-dollar now. Eden has a few, too, that are growing. Cassie said they meant immunity. That means the baby should be immune, too, right?"

Shax nodded, not looking away from the baby.

Garrett's eyes went wide. "Did you see that? When she opened her eyes?"

"Her eyes are a mix of mine and Angel's," Shax said. "One blue and one green and yellow."

Garret and I shared a look. I didn't know what it meant that a baby who, by all accounts, wasn't Shax's biological baby had some of his attributes. So instead, I focused on what I did know.

The baby was healthy and alert, and Angel had survived the birth.

That meant I'd probably survive mine too.

The future was coming, whether I was ready or not. And it no longer sounded as terrifying as I'd thought it had.

I looked up at Scath as Shax and Garrett headed for the door.

"Are you ready to go home?" I asked.

He kissed my forehead.

"Yes. Let's go home. There is still a wall you haven't tried."

I shook my head. "That's what got me into this mess."

"Not a mess," he said. "No matter what our baby looks like, it will be ours, and we will love it."

He was right. We would. Unconditionally, just like I knew Shax and Angel, and everyone else in Tolerance, would love hers.

Thank you for reading *Demon Blind*!
If you're ready for more, be sure to check out *Demon Defeat: Part Two*.

AUTHOR'S NOTE

Where to start? Let's see... I was working on Demon Defeat, plotting away, when this little side story started nibbling at my mind. I tried to ignore it. Who has time for a side novella when there's a pre-order deadline for the series finale? Definitely not me.

Unfortunately, my easily distracted self did not cooperate with the big-picture game plan. I told myself it would be a super short story. It's not. I told myself it wouldn't take me long. A week, maybe two tops. It took way longer. And I told myself it was okay to take a short detour because I would have plenty of time to finish Demon Defeat on time.

Demon Defeat was half-written and six days overdue to my editor at this point.

So I told myself it'll be okay. The fans truly wanted more fey, and if I squeezed in another novella, they wouldn't be horribly angry if I had to push back Demon Defeat's release by a few weeks.

I didn't just push back the release...I woefully underestimated how much story there was to tell and had to split the finale into two parts. Which is why Angel's childbirth is here. Don't worry! You'll see more of the gang in Demon Defeat: Part 2!

Hopefully, you found this side story and the delays it caused worthwhile. I can't wait to share the conclusion of the Resurrection Chronicles with you.

Until next time, happy reading!
Melissa

THE
RESURRECTION CHRONICLES

Humor, romance, and sexy dark fey!

BOOK 1: DEMON EMBER

In a world going to hell, Mya must learn to accept help from her new-found demon protector in order to find her family as a zombie-like plague spreads.

BOOK 2: DEMON FLAMES

As hellhounds continue to roam and the zombie plague spreads, Drav leads Mya to the source of her troubles—Ernisi, an underground Atlantis and Drav's home. There Mya learns that the shadowy demons, who've helped devastate her world, are not what they seem.

BOOK 3: DEMON ASH

While in Ernisi, cites were been bombed and burned in an attempt to stop the plague. Now, Marauders, hellhounds, and the infected are doing their best to destroy what's left of the world. It's up to Mya and Drav to save it.

BOOK 4: DEMON ESCAPE

While running from zombies, hellhounds, and the people who kept her prisoner, Eden encounters a new creature. He claims he only wants to protect her. Eden must decide who the real devils are between man and demon, and choosing wrong could cost her life.

BOOK 5: DEMON DECEPTION

Grieving from the loss of her husband and youngest child, Cassie lives in fear of losing her remaining daughter. To gain protection, Cassie knows she needs to sleep with one of the dark fey and give him the one thing she isn't sure she can. Her heart.

THE RESURRECTION CHRONICLES

The apocalyptic adventure continues!

BOOK 6: DEMON NIGHT

Angel's growing weaker by the day and needs help. In exchange for food, she agrees to give Shax advice regarding how to win over Hannah. If Angel can help make that happen, just maybe she won't be kicked out when her fellow survivors find out she's pregnant.

BOOK 7: DEMON DAWN

In a post-apocalyptic world, Benna is faced with the choice of trading her body and heart to the dark fey in order to survive the infected.

BOOK 8: DEMON DISGRACE

Hannah is drinking away her life to stanch the bleeding pain from past trauma. Merdon, a dark fey with a violent history, relentlessly sets out to show her there's something worth living for.

BOOK 9: DEMON FALL

June never planned to fall in love. She had her eyes on the prize: a career and independence. Too bad the world ended and stole those options from her. Maybe falling in love had been the better choice after all.

The Beastly Tales

Beauty and the Beast with seductively dark twists!

Book 1: Depravity

When impoverished, beautiful Benella is locked inside the dark and magical estate of the beast, she must bargain for her freedom if she wants to see her family again.

Book 2: Deceit

Safely hidden within the estate's enchanted walls, Benella no longer has time to fear her tormentors. She's too preoccupied trying to determine what makes the beast so beastly. In order to gain her freedom, she must find a way to break the curse, but first, she must help him become a better man while protecting her heart.

Book 3: Devastation

Abused and rejected, Benella strives to regain a purpose for her life, and finds herself returning to the last place she ever wanted to see. She must learn when it is right to forgive and when it is time to move on.

TALES OF CINDER

Be careful what you wish for...

PREQUEL: DISOWNED

In a world where the measure of a person rarely goes beneath the surface, Margaret Thoning refuses to play by its rules. She walks away from everything she's ever known to risk her heart and her life for the people who matter most.

BOOK 1: DEFIANT

When the sudden death of Eloise's mother points to forbidden magic, Eloise's life quickly goes from fairy tale to nightmare. Kaven, the prince's manservant, is Eloise's prime suspect. However, when dark magic is used, nothing is as simple as it seems.

BOOK 2: DISDAIN

Cursed to silence, Eloise is locked in the tattered remains of her once charming life. The smoldering spark of her anger burns for answers and revenge. However, games of magic can have dire consequences.

BOOK 3: DAMNATION

With the reason behind her mother's death revealed, Eloise must prevent her stepsisters from marrying the prince and exact her revenge. However, a secret of the royal court strikes a blow to her plans. Betrayed, Eloise will question how far she's willing to go for revenge.

Made in the USA
Las Vegas, NV
04 December 2023

82097329R00135